Range
of No Return

Range
of No Return

A Western Duo

D. B. Newton

Five Star • Waterville, Maine

First Edition
First Printing: December, 2005

Published in 2005 in conjunction with Tekno Books and Ed Gorman.

Set in 11 pt. Plantin.

Printed in the United States on permanent paper.

Library of Congress Cataloging-in-Publication Data

Newton, D. B. (Dwight Bennett), 1916–
   [Claim jumpers]
   Range of no return : a western duo / D. B. Newton.—1st ed.
    p. cm.
   ISBN 1-59414-159-2 (hc : alk. paper)
   1. Western stories.   I. Newton, D. B. (Dwight Bennett), 1916–
Range of no return. II. Title.
PS3527.E9178C57 2005
813'.52—dc22   2005023725

Table of Contents

Foreword
by
Jon Tuska

D. B. Newton is the author of an impressive body of Western fiction, but his visibility among readers has been compromised in large part over the years by his having written books under six different names. He was born in Kansas City, Missouri on January 14, 1916 and was educated in elementary and secondary schools in Kansas City. In 1937 he entered the University of Missouri in that city, receiving his Bachelor's degree in 1940 and his Master's degree in history and political science in 1942. He had not yet completed the work for his advanced degree when in 1941 he married Mary Jane Kregel. Two children, both daughters, resulted from this union.

Newton always wanted to be a writer. His first published piece, a poem, was printed on the reader's page of a religious magazine titled *Wee Wisdom* when he was eight. At twelve he came upon an issue of Street & Smith's *Western Story Magazine* and it was a couple of stories by Max Brand that he read at this time that convinced him he had found the kind of fiction he wanted to write himself. He started right in and a decade later, when he was a sophomore in college, his first 12,000-word novelette was accepted by a Red Circle pulp in the Newsstand group. It appeared under the title "Brand of the Hunted" in *Western Novel and Short Stories* (7/38). In it, Rex Mahan flees after a shooting that is in self-defense and, as the story opens, is on his way back to Crown Point to turn himself in when he is ambushed on the trail. His horse is shot but he downs the ambusher. A badge in the man's

pocket, $10,000 in bank money in his saddlebags, and pos-
session of Sheriff Ed Whitaker's small gelding convince Rex
that he now has killed a lawman. He strikes out on the sheriff's horse. When he arrives in the border town of Mesquite,
his conscience has got the better of him and he decides to
return the money, writing a note to the bank in Crown Point
and leaving the loot in the hotel safe. Before he can get away,
he is captured by the town marshal's daughter who is also the
marshal's only deputy. When the owner of the hotel hides the
money, Polly Haines, the marshal's daughter, proposes to her
father that they let Mahan escape so he can recover it himself
since they cannot prove the hotel owner stole it. This episode
is rather preposterous and Mahan might easily have been
killed in the ensuing confrontation, to say nothing of all the
laws that are bent by the marshal in gathering evidence, but
on another level, that of the essential decency of a number of
the characters in the story, the narrative concludes in a mood
of moral affirmation.

Six months later a novelette by Newton titled "Range
Where Men Died Twice" appeared in *Western Short Stories*
(12/38) followed by a short story "Gunshot Granger" also in
Western Short Stories (5/39). He had been paid $60 for "Brand
of the Hunted" and by the end of his first year had earned
$137. During the decade between when he first read *Western
Story Magazine* and when he published his first Western fiction, Newton had read widely in the field. These early stories
are obviously more derivative than original. "Gunshot
Granger" depends on a twist at the end in the best O. Henry
fashion and incorporates the "kingpin" principle so common
to Ernest Haycox's fiction in the 1930s—remove the chief in-
stigator and peace is restored.

Newton continued to write for the pulp market until he
completed his degree work in 1942 at which time he entered

military service and was assigned to the U.S. Army Corps of Engineers. Surveying the titles of his contributions to the magazine market from 1938 until the time he left the service, there seems to be little hiatus. This is deceptive. He had acted as his own agent until early 1941 when an editor recommended him as a promising new writer to Marguerite E. Harper, agent for T. T. Flynn, Luke Short, and Peter Dawson. Harper was a forceful person who wanted her clients to write fast and prodigiously. Newton was not ready for her and actually gave up writing for a year to earn his Master's degree with the idea of entering teaching. He took up writing again, though, and continued to write in his spare time while in the service. In 1946 he resumed civilian life, now determined to make his living free-lancing full time for the magazine markets. August Lenniger had become his agent in 1944. This was a mixed blessing. When starting out, Newton had remained with the Newsstand group. In 1940 he began appearing in *.44 Western* and, later, *Ace-High Western* and *Big-Book Western*, published by Popular Publications. By 1945 he was also to be found in the Ace group and the next year, with the appearance of "Smoke-Pole Rendezvous in Abilene" in *Lariat Story Magazine* (7/46), he broke into the Fiction House group. This was auspicious since Fiction House was a market Harper ignored and yet Newton would produce some of his best fiction for it. In common with L.P. Holmes whose first short story had appeared in a Fiction House magazine, Newton regarded his occupation as a magazine writer satisfying as long as he enjoyed what he was writing and was happy to deal with editors who were pleased with what he wrote as opposed to striving constantly after the better-paying slick markets. Norman A. Fox agreed and subsequently wrote to Newton about his friend and fellow Montanan, A. B. Guthrie, Jr., who had chosen the other course.

"I've watched Bud struggling through the years," Fox observed, "forced to try and keep on topping himself. I'd rather be D. B. Newton!" Newton did set challenges for himself, but, overall, in his own words: "I simply tried to do the best job I could, on the kind of Western I would have enjoyed reading if Luke Short or Haycox had written it."

Captain Joseph T. Shaw, a former editor of *Black Mask* magazine turned agent, encouraged his clients such as Dan Cushman and Frank Bonham to establish personal relationships with editors. Lenniger did not believe in it. As a consequence, Newton never had any direct contact with Malcolm Reiss while the latter was principal editor and general manager at Fiction House. However, Reiss knew Newton's work well enough that, when he invited him to contribute a book-length manuscript for *Two Western Books* and Newton sent in a short outline, Reiss could tell Lenniger, after accepting it: "Newton usually knows what he's doing." However, not all editors were of the same opinion. Jack O'Sullivan, when he joined Reiss's editorial staff at Fiction House, sent a memo to Lenniger in which he defined what he termed the "D. B. Newton problem". "I would liken a Newton story," O'Sullivan stated, "to a nice, thick rope that gradually dwindles down into a string." This so-called "problem" is apparent in "Smoke-Pole Rendezvous in Abilene", where Dan Paris, a Kansas farmer, finds his wife and newborn baby killed and his crops ruined due to a cattle stampede during a rainstorm. He sets out for revenge and is arrested by Wild Bill Hickok before he is able to shoot the arrogant trail boss who, he believes, killed his family. When Hickok questions the trail boss, the latter claims not to know Paris. When Paris is released by Hickok, he is hired by saloon man Phil Coe. Paris finds he has a natural talent as a gambler. He makes friends with June Williams, who is being courted by the trail boss,

10

and he witnesses the gun battle between Hickok and Coe in which Coe is mortally wounded and Hickok's close friend, Mike Williams, is accidentally shot by Hickok. Paris prevents two men from killing Hickok, and then, after this, decides that vengeance is a useless and self-defeating emotion. Rather he will return to his farm and start once more to build a future. On his way to call on June, Mike Williams's sister, he passes the trail boss on the road and does not even look at him twice.

Newton once observed that "while I respected Frank Bonham, Dan Cushman, and other talented people who seemed to be consciously trying to raise the level of pulp fiction through the sheer quality of their individual work, I secretly felt they were probably wasting their time. As long as the publishers were satisfied to trash their own magazines with the kind of embarrassingly bad cover art that had forced me, as a twelve-year-old, to hide *Western Story Magazine* under my shirt on my way home from the drugstore, no reader with any taste was ever likely to know—or care to know—what might be inside them. . . ." This statement is not to be taken at full value, though, since Newton in his own way provided Fiction House with a significant number of stories that are of lasting interest precisely because they are off-trail, because they do have the "D. B. Newton problem" and avoid all the more compulsory traditional elements that characterize so much lower-grade pulp fiction. Among them, surely, are "Born to the Brand" from *Lariat Story Magazine* (9/46), collected in *Born to the Brand* (Five Star Westerns, 2001); "On Treachery Trail" from *Frontier Stories* (Winter, 46) for its sympathetic treatment of Mormons; "Reach High, Tophand!" from *Lariat Story Magazine* (7/47), also collected in *Born to the Brand*; "Riders of Vengeance Trail" from *Frontier Stories* (Winter, 48) which seizes a reader viscerally from the very beginning and is weakened at the conclusion only by the obligatory fight scene the editor insisted be inserted; and "Stage Coach West" from *Frontier Stories* (Spring, 52) which vividly recreates stage travel as notably as Frank Bonham could. These stories, as well as others in Fiction House and Popular Publications magazines, are undermined only by their titles, often provided by the editors whose garish whimsy never failed them. "All the characters in the novelette are real people—even the villain," Lenniger wrote to Newton after reading the first story he submitted to the agency. "You always come up with heroes about whom one can *care*." Actually what makes Newton's Western fiction so special is a combination of characters who seem real and about whom a reader comes to care a great deal and Newton's fundamental humanity, his realization early on (perhaps because of his study of history) that little that happened in the West was ever simple but rather made desperately complicated through the conjunction of numerous opposed forces working at cross-purposes. Yet through all of the turmoil on the frontier a basic human decency did emerge. It was this that made the American frontier experience so profoundly unique and produced a heritage of remarkable human beings of which the nation they built could be proud, always. Newton knew this and it elevates his magazine fiction to a level that demands the best of it be preserved permanently, and these are the same qualities which also characterize so many of his subsequent novels.

Newton had grown up in a border state. He came to Oregon for the first time during the Second World War. In 1943 he and his wife bought a home in Bend, in Oregon's high desert. In 1949, due to Bend's increasing population and the tug of family relations, the Newtons sold out and moved back to Kansas City. By 1952 they had moved again, to Santa Barbara, only then to move back to Bend where they acquired the house next door to the one they had previously owned. Except for the time Newton spent in Los Angeles writing for television during which period the Bend home was rented out, Bend would remain his home.

In 1948 Lenniger further expanded Newton's magazine markets so that occasionally he would appear in *Western Story* (in fact, his was the last story in the last issue of this magazine in 1949) and far more often in Standard Magazines. Samuel Mines, an editor at Standard Magazines, remarked about Newton that "sometimes he's good, and sometimes he's pretty hack." Probably the chief determining factor was the market for which Newton was writing. If it was a cover novel for *Rio Kid Western*, *Masked Rider Western*, or *Texas Rangers*, Newton had a tendency to rely on melodrama and the obvious, predictable resolution to a conflict in the plot. There was only a very limited amount of characterization in one of these superhero pulp novels because the principals were all trademarked by the magazine for which the story was being written. Newton's frustration in writing superhero stories is more evident than elsewhere when he might only have to rewrite an ending to avoid the "D. B. Newton problem". Perhaps for a similar reason, Newton's first efforts at producing Western novels are disappointing compared to his later work. The first two—*Guns of the Rimrock* (Phoenix Press, 1946) and *The Gunmaster of Saddleback* (Phoenix Press, 1948)—are very much in the routine tradition of novels produced for this lending-library publisher by Walker A. Tompkins, Leslie Scott, and T. W. Ford. In fact, *The Trigger Slammer* (Phoenix Press, 1946) by T. W. Ford bears a title more evocative of what was wanted, although Newton's titles do at least incorporate that almost obligatory word—gun.

The breakthrough came with Newton's third novel, *Range Boss* (Pocket Books, 1949). It is an expansion of "Gunhawk's Kid" from *Western Novel and Short Stories* (12/47). Originally Newton had titled this story *The Trail Beyond Boothill*, a title the British hard cover edition, published by Samson and Low, retained. The magazine version came about because Lenniger had had a rush order for a 35,000-word story from the magazine's editor and Newton obliged by abridging the novel he was working on between stories. It was the editor's idea to change the title even though there is no "gunhawk", much less a "kid" anywhere in the narrative. Then, no longer faced by a magazine deadline, Newton at his leisure went back and wrote this novel the way he had intended to write it. When he sent it to Lenniger, he fully expected it to be sent on to Phoenix Press that was paying him a flat $150 a book, no royalties. Recently Pocket Books had done well with its reprint of a lending library Western novel, L.P. Holmes's *Flame of Sunset* (Samuel Curl, 1947). The quality of Holmes's novel was definitely atypical and should never have been sold to such a market in the first place. However, Lenniger did not make that mistake with Newton's new novel. He sent it to Pocket Books directly where it was accepted, retitled *Range Boss*, and would appear as the first *original* Western novel to be published by Pocket Books. It was so successful it sold over 450,000 copies, in contrast to a Phoenix book which seldom exceeded 2,000 units, the usual press run, and which was never reprinted by the firm but only offered for paperback reprint. Understandably, hard cover publishers were not enthusiastic about a paperback reprint company entering the field of publishing original Western fiction and they forced Pocket Books to retreat, at least for a time, by threatening to withhold reprint rights on titles Pocket Books wished to acquire. *Range*

Boss remains memorable for the old-timers who enter the story about halfway through, reminiscent in their way of the old-timers in Walt Coburn's early novels. In Newton's case this was a proclivity. As he himself aged, his characters in the second half of life became ever more vivid and affecting.

Newton's next three novels were all for hard cover publishers. All three had first appeared in magazine versions and all three were eventually published in paperback reprints. *Shotgun Guard* (Lippincott, 1950) is a novel very much in the Ernest Haycox and Luke Short tradition with a complex plot, the theme of the two heroines (which one is right for the hero only emerging after the main conflict has been resolved), and a mystery element: who is backing the competing stage line and who murdered its foremost promoter? The events in the plot are slightly compromised by elements of melodrama, but the story does have many intriguing elements. *Stormy Range* (Doubleday, 1951) was Newton's fifth novel, and his first to appear as a Double D. Because of the protest lodged by Doubleday when Les Savage, Jr., used his own name on an original Fawcett Gold Medal paperback Western after having published two Double D Westerns, Lenniger decided that henceforth his clients would have to use different names every time their books were bought by a different publisher. Some clients, such as Clifton Adams, quit the agency over the practice. *Stormy Range* was published under the byline Dwight Bennett, as henceforth would be all of Newton's Double D Westerns. The protagonist is Clem Hardin who inherits the great Ladder ranch. When Newton wrote the first of what would be a series of twelve novels for editor Donald A. Wollheim at Ace Books, *Hellbent for a Hangrope* (Ace, 1954), he chose as his byline Clement Hardin. In some quarters, because of the massive circulation of an Ace paperback, this name became a more familiar one

15

than either D. B. Newton or Dwight Bennett. *Six-Gun Gamble* (Lippincott, 1951) was again under the D. B. Newton byline. It would prove his last novel for Lippincott. When *Fire in the Desert* (Ballantine, 1954) appeared, Newton was assigned yet another byline, Ford Logan, and beginning with *Outlaw River* (Popular Library, 1955), he acquired still one more: Dan Temple.

In pulp magazines when an author had two stories appearing in the same issue, he was often assigned a house name for one of them, as when "Three from the Dark Trails" in *.44 Western* (3/43) under the byline D. B. Newton and "Never Too Old to Fight", also by Newton in the same issue, carried the byline Dave Sand. However, in book publishing to have so many different bylines tended to diminish Newton's recognition among readers. By contrast, Luke Short and Peter Dawson were the bylines used respectively by Fred and Jon Glidden. Everything Fred Glidden wrote carried the Luke Short byline. Everything Jon Glidden wrote carried the Peter Dawson byline. Lenniger's mania for multiple bylines persisted long after publishers abandoned any claim to "ownership" of a byline (having realized that the more ubiquitous a byline the higher its visibility and the author's marketability). This hurt Newton as also did Lenniger's policy of regarding a Western novel the equivalent of a pulp story so that, after its first publication, its value as a property virtually ceased. The lack of an aggressive effort to keep Newton's books in print, as was the case early on with Ernest Haycox and Luke Short and a number of others including Louis L'Amour, all of whose novels were kept constantly in print, unfairly limited his income from what he did publish.

In 1957, Frank Gruber invited Newton to contribute scripts to his "Tales of Wells Fargo" television series. This marked the beginning of a three-year hiatus from writing books and from a pulp magazine market that had all but collapsed. Newton went on to contribute scripts to other television series such as "Wagon Train" and "Death Valley Days". Tired of the stresses of television scriptwriting by 1960 and longing to return to Oregon, Newton resumed writing novels. Lenniger warned him that he had been away for a time, that the editors had changed, and that it would be the same as starting anew. However, within a year he was again well established. Lenniger suggested to Berkley Books that Newton would be ideal, with his television connections, to author a book series about a continuing character. Newton had developed a series idea for Chuck Connors that did not come to fruition because Connors began starring in "The Rifleman" television series instead. Newton's character was named Jim Bannister and he became the continuing character in the eleven-volume Bannister series.

From Newton's early period as a novelist, his best work can be found in his Double D Westerns as Dwight Bennett. In addition, *Top Hand* (Perma Books, 1955), an expansion of "Reach High, Tophand!" and published by a then Doubleday paperback subsidiary, is no less fine and a comparison of the novelette version and the expansion demonstrates just how seamlessly Newton could weave a second group of characters into the basic storyline, giving a more definite sense of place (in the novel the location is the John Day country in Oregon), and providing numerous characters with an added depth of personality. *Hellbent for a Hangrope* was an auspicious beginning for his first Ace entry under the Clement Hardin byline and it is notable for its locations in Kansas and the Nations and its use of historical personalities such as Belle Starr, Sam Starr, and Bat Masterson.

Newton's later period really begins with *Cherokee Outlet* (Doubleday, 1961) and, if anything, the years of experience, historical study, and a deepening concern for the human condition raise his Double D Westerns between this novel and *Disaster Creek* (Doubleday, 1981) to a level of consistent accomplishment achieved by only a few of his peers. The Oregon settings of so many of his finest novels—Prineville in *Crooked River Canyon* (Doubleday, 1966), Canyon City in *The Big Land* (Doubleday, 1972), and the small town of Mitchell in 1904 in *Disaster Creek*—and the communities he created are evoked with an ambient glow equaled, but not surpassed, by L. P. Holmes in those novels Holmes set in the Napa Valley of northern California. In novels such as *The Big Land*, in which Chief Paulina and his band of renegade Snakes are characterized no less than the Wasco and Warm Springs Indians who scouted for the pursuing whites, Newton provided a tapestry that vividly renders the complex social forces that had inevitably to clash in the struggle between these various cultures to survive in an environment made more volatile by irreconcilable differences in perspective. The "D. B. Newton problem" works to both the author's and the reader's advantage in these novels, so that turnings in the plot are seldom predictable. There are increasingly no heroes, heroines, or villains in these novels, just flawed human beings who are crippled or compromised by their own shortcomings. Newton's female characters, from Emily Bishop in *The Big Land* to Kit Tracy in *Disaster Creek*, are memorable for their delicate characterization, their warm-heartedness, and their spirited resolve combined with personal capability.

Many Western writers seem to have a Golden Age, a period during which they produce their best work. In this, along with such authors as Les Savage, Jr., Will Cook, and Frank Bonham, Newton's passage would appear to be one of linear ascent, with only an occasional setback, so that in general and gradually he became better and better. He may not have set out to do this consciously, the way A. B. Guthrie, Jr., or Jack Schaefer did, but the result was the same. Even his ground-breaking entries in the "Stagecoach" series under the Bantam Books house name Hank Mitchum remain the best in that necessarily variable series. It might justifiably be stated—had he not had quite so many bylines—that a D. B. Newton novel can almost always be counted on to provide Western fiction of the highest quality, historically accurate and balanced in perspective, with involving characters and situations, all of it informed by an encompassing humanity. As it stands presently, all reprints of his work and his new books for the Five Star Westerns are under the name D. B. Newton, and the assessment remains.

One of the founding members of the Western Writers of America and for many years the organization's secretary-treasurer, Newton in his own way, because of his innate interest in Western writers and Western fiction, became the unofficial historian for the genre, and, while he himself wrote little on the subject, his opinions and knowledge were frequently consulted by others. Newton once recalled how, after he had completed "Reach High, Tophand!" and started to read the story aloud to his wife, he found her weeping halfway through it. Forty-five years after he wrote it, he commented on that story that it no longer seemed "even particularly well-written, though it was the best prose anyone could expect out of me in 1946. . . . Still, after all these years, it's nice to think that once at least the magic worked—and with the one person in the world I was most anxious that it should! I'm willing to settle for that."

The Claim Jumpers

I

Bill Emery suggested, without much conviction: "I suppose there's still a chance he'll show up in time?"

"Why kid ourselves?" old Mac McIvor grunted scornfully, and shook his grizzled head. "I heard one of them Army fellers sayin' they calculate there's sixty thousand of us strung out along the line, waiting for the signal tomorrow. You figure Johnny Haig is going to locate one blamed campfire in such a mess as this?"

Emery stabbed his fork into his tin plate of biscuits and beans, then suddenly set the works on the ground beside him, appetite failing. "Why didn't we arrange things better? We could have named a place to meet, just in case we missed connections at Caldwell."

"Johnny wouldn't have made it no-how. You savvy the way he is when he gets going on one of his binges. He'll likely be sleeping it off in some Dodge City hotel about now."

Ed Coulton, who had been silent for a long time during their disheartened talk, unhitched his lanky frame and, getting to his feet, dumped tin plate and cup into the wreck pan, having spilled out the last dregs of coffee.

"I figure it's all my fault," he said gloomily, as he dug into his shirt pocket for tobacco and papers. "I should have kept better track of him, the night we went through Dodge, and not let myself get involved in that stud game at Morgan Banning's clip joint. After they cleaned me, I looked high and low for Johnny but no use . . . I couldn't find him. There was no choice but to come on without him."

"Nobody's blaming anybody," said old McIvor. "It's just too danged bad . . . because we planned everything so careful,

23

and we need all four of us to make it work."

Bill Emery suggested: "Maybe we can pick up somebody to take Johnny's place?"

"Who? Who you going to find that we can trust in this land-crazy mob of wild men?"

Bill had to admit: "I don't know."

"Aw, the devil. Pass me the jug, somebody," muttered Ed Coulton.

Bill Emery wasn't interested in the jug or its contents, however. Instead of joining his friends in a drink, he left them and walked away alone through that clutter of camps crowding an invisible boundary.

Mac had said 60,000—60,000 jostling, high-spirited people, lured from every corner of the country by the call of free land—waiting for the rifle shot at noon tomorrow which would mark the greatest rush in history. The Cherokee Strip—there for the taking, open to any who could first get stakes into sod and make their claims stick. Tonight it was a vast expanse of virgin soil; by this time tomorrow every acre would be claimed and marked out in homestead tracts.

Emery walked among the close-scattered camps of the land-rushers, looking a little out of place in his tall cowboy boots and hat. Every man he saw was either a townsman or a farmer. If any noticed Bill Emery, they probably wondered that a cowpuncher should take any interest in this event that was destined to convert the last cattle range of the Indian Nations into farmsteads and end, forever, the days of free graze.

The cattlemen, their Cherokee leases outlawed by the government, had long since taken their herds and moved farther West. Why, these people were likely wondering, hadn't he gone with them?

Bill, in return, felt a kind of amazement at the optimism

and poor sense of these hopefuls, many of whom had brought their wives and children. Without adequate provisions, with no knowledge of the land they hoped to find, they merely counted on luck to get them a good place to sink their stakes. And there could be a dozen contestants for every available claim.

Meanwhile, to everything else was added the hot, choking discomfort of a September drought that had clamped tightly over this sweltering border country, baking the Kansas plains to sun-cracked scabs. Yonder, a man had a barrel of water in a wagon and was doling it out to a yelling, shoving lineup of pilgrims at a dollar a cup. Bill's mouth worked with distaste. He knew what the stuff would taste like—gyp water, foul, scarcely palatable. He walked on. He wasn't that thirsty. Not yet.

At a small booth, a long queue of Strippers was headed up—a line that moved but slowly through the thick dust, and the unbearable heat that remained even though the sun lay low on the flat horizon. They were registering for the run tomorrow, and no doubt the booth would remain open all of this last night.

It was a futile scheme some genius in the Land Office had thought up, in an attempt to thwart the Sooners that were known to have evaded the military by the hundreds and sneaked onto the Strip ahead of time. Actually it meant only an additional quota of suffering for everybody; Bill Emery's own certificate was buttoned in his shirt pocket, and it had taken exactly three hours in the sun to wait out his turn and collect it.

He was so busied with these sour thoughts that he did not realize anyone was speaking to him until a hand plucked at his sleeve. He looked around. The girl was an uncommonly pretty one, and she was startlingly close to him—so near that,

25

in turning, his arm touched the soft swell of her bosom and he stepped back quickly. He scowled, and said gruffly: "Look, I got too many things on my mind. . . ."

He saw her turn pink, to the roots of her soft black hair. At the same time he realized the full size of his error. There were plenty of such women working this huge mob of rootless, excitement-hunting men—but she was not one of them.

She wasn't dressed like those others, in their bedraggled, dust-grimed finery; she did not reek of their perfume, or carry the inevitable frilled parasol to shield the smashing sunlight from a white and painted face. This girl wore a simple skirt and blouse, and her face and throat were beaded with honest perspiration, while her high color was that of pure embarrassment. She stammered—"I . . . I. . . ."—and then abruptly she whirled away from him.

"Please!" cried Bill Emery, blurting it out. "I'm sorry as the devil, ma'am! I apologize for thinking. . . . Listen, is there anything I can do?" For in that instant of meeting her eyes he had read in them worry and a near desperation.

He thought she wasn't going to answer. But she halted, forcing herself to turn. She said, in a muffled tone: "I've lost a team of horses. I was going to ask if you'd seen them."

"Horses?" he echoed. "Why, no. I ain't noticed none running loose."

"They weren't loose. Some . . . somebody took them, while I was in line at the registration booth. I had them tied to my wagon wheel." She nodded toward a rig that he could see parked not far away from where they stood. "When I got back just now, they were gone. I'd tied the knots good and strong. I know they couldn't have broken away."

Bill's face darkened. "Well, they're gone for good then. You should have known better than to leave anything around with this crazy mob. Horseflesh is at a premium and you can take it for granted you'll never lay eyes on those bronc's again!" He saw this hit her, hard, saw her mouth begin to tremble.

"But I . . . there wasn't anyone I could leave them with," she protested. On the last word her voice broke and she suddenly whirled from him and went at a run toward the stranded wagon. She vanished from sight, around the wagon box. Bill Emery was left staring.

He couldn't move, for a moment or so. Then something drew him after the girl, and, rounding the wagon, he saw that she had put her face against the tailboard and was weeping openly. He stood helplessly, but deeply concerned.

"Look, ma'am," he blurted, "you don't really mean that you're out here all by yourself? You surely must have a . . . a husband, or folks, or something?"

"I've got folks," she told him in a muffled voice, raising her head. "My mother, and three little sisters. That's all I have in the world . . . and I'm bound on taking out land and bringing them here to try and make a home for them! I've *got* to!" She broke off into sobs. It was like the crying of a little girl.

Numb and uncomfortable, Bill Emery looked around him. It was not much of a camp. The wagon held a small leather chest, brass-bound, a few meager supplies. The girl did not even have a fire built—was apparently too dazed with grief to think of this, or of getting herself anything to eat.

Automatically he set about gathering materials and got a small blaze to burning. When he had this done, he dug up a coffee pot from the stuff in the wagon, got a little water from a spare supply in the wagon canteen, and set coffee to brewing. As he straightened from shoving more wood into the blaze, he saw the girl standing nearby, watching him. The warm light showed an odd and sober expression on her face.

"What are you doing?" she demanded.

"You'll feel better if you get some food in you."

She pulled at her lower lip with small, white teeth. "Thank you," she said finally. "I guess I sort of lost my head. I'll behave myself now."

With that promise, she took over preparing her own meal, and Bill Emery stood aside and watched her quick movements in silence. But when she brought two tin cups from the wagon, he said: "Whoa up! I've already eaten. I wasn't promoting myself any grub."

She looked at him, giving him her whole attention for the first time. "Who are you?"

"Cowpoke. The name is Bill Emery."

"I'm . . . Laura Cain." It didn't occur to him until later that she maybe hesitated a fraction of a second in giving the name. She asked: "Are you going to stake a homestead tomorrow?"

"Figure to." Eyes hooded, Bill was working on the fashioning of a smoke. He looked at the girl, who sat on the ground opposite him with a plate on her knee, eating with real appetite. As he snapped a match to fire his smoke, Bill studied her, remembering what she had told him, and seeing how alone and defenseless she seemed, here without friends.

"Look!" he exclaimed in sudden decision and as her big, dark eyes lifted to his own. "Even if you had your horses back, you wouldn't stand a chance in a million tomorrow, going it alone. But maybe I can show you something really worthwhile. You'll have to promise, though," he added, "to do exactly as I tell you."

"I . . . don't understand," she faltered. "I hope you don't mean . . . ?" Her eyes darkened, turning sharp and unfriendly.

He reddened. "I'm sorry. I apologize again for thinking . . . for the mistake I made. Honest, I got no intention of hurting you. Neither will my friends. There's three of us," he hurried on. "There was supposed to be a fourth, but we've lost him and we'll need someone to take his place if our plan is to work. I'd sort of like to count you in, Laura. Of course, you understand the others will have to give their approval."

"What is it you want me to do?"

"Here, I'll show you." Quickly Bill Emery smoothed the dirt between them with the flat of his hand, and began to trace a map as he talked. "Me and these three friends of mine . . . Mac McIvor, Ed Coulton, and Johnny Haig . . . we rode for the Figure Eight outfit, punching cattle on graze our boss leased from the Cherokee Nation. We know the Strip by heart . . . every hill and gully, and thicket of wild plum, and acre of buffalo grass. It's a beautiful country . . . or *was!* After tomorrow, though, when these sodbusters come swarming all over, putting up wire and tearing the land to pieces with their plows . . . well, that ain't a sight I'm looking forward to, since I'll be remembering what it used to be like."

She looked puzzled. "But you said you were taking out a homestead . . . ?"

"I ain't aiming to stay on it, any longer'n it takes to sell out at a profit and head West, where there's still room for a man to breathe. Here's the deal." He made his markings in the dust with a rope-hardened forefinger.

"This is Cherry Creek. An old Indian trail crosses it . . . so. And here's the Figure Eight headquarters. When the government ordered the cattle companies out of the Strip, all improvements were supposed to have been torn down. Any they left, the military was to have destroyed before the opening tomorrow. But through some oversight, the Figure Eight buildings were missed. I slipped across the line a couple of days ago just to make sure, and they're standing the way we left them . . . the barns, the bunkhouse, everything. A prize, for whoever grabs it off."

The girl nodded seriously. "I guess I can see that. A house and all . . . ready to move right in."

"But that's not the main thing. The way the government surveyors worked it out, there's a corner marker right in the middle of the pasture, north of the ranch. Those four quarter-sections command the ranch headquarters, the Cherry Creek bottoms, and the crossing. Supply trains to old Oklahoma have used that Indian trail for years, it being the one good fording place on the creek. Sooner or later, a railroad will follow it. And right there . . ."—he stabbed his finger hard into the crude map he'd traced—"sure as shooting, a town is gonna grow. It's bound to! We just have to go through the legality of setting up a town site company and registering the plat at the county seat, and start selling lots. We'll all of us be rich before we're finished."

"I see."

He thought she sounded dubious. "I tell you, everything's in our favor. We know the country, we know the very place we mean to drop our stakes. We got good, fast cow ponies to carry us. All that will give us an advantage that these others will have a hard time beating. Only one thing is wrong. Johnny Haig has turned up missing. So we need somebody else to come in with us, and stake that fourth corner. Would you be interested?"

He stubbed out his cigarette, giving her time to consider.

"I . . . I don't know what to say," Laura Cain told him finally. "What makes you think that you can trust me . . . a stranger?"

"It's a chance, with anybody we pick out to take Johnny's place. I'd be willing to risk it on you."

"But I'm not sure that I. . . ."

"Can trust me?"

She colored faintly. "That isn't what I started to say. I meant that I'm not sure we're after the same things. I'm not looking for property I can sell for a lot of money. I want a home."

"Farming a quarter section of prairie land? Without even a man to help you?" Emery shook his head. "You don't know what you're talking about. You'd make out a lot better living in a town . . . especially if you was to own a fourth interest in the town company."

"No!" cried Laura Cain, with a sudden fierceness that startled him. "I've seen enough of towns! I want none of them, for myself or my sisters, not after. . . ." She caught herself, left the thing unfinished. And Bill Emery, with a shrug, climbed to his feet.

"Well, have it your way," he grunted. "It was just a suggestion." He looked around the wagon camp, back to the girl. "Whatever you do, you're gonna have to travel light if you hope to get anything tomorrow. . . . I tell you what," he added on an impulse born of the solemn despair in Laura Cain's pretty, sunburned face. "Can you sit a stock saddle?" And at her nod: "Happens I got an extra pony . . . a zippy little dun mare that can run rings around 'most anything on legs, excepting my old piebald. I'll let you use her. I know some spots, 'twixt here and Figure Eight that would make likely enough homesteads. You ride with me tomorrow, and maybe I can drop you off at one of them on the way. All right?"

It was her turn to rise, facing him, a look almost of disbelief in her eyes. "You'd really do this? When you know I couldn't repay you?"

" 'Sall right," he grunted, and started to turn away. "I reckon I ain't selfish enough not to help somebody when they need it bad, and it wouldn't be any particular trouble."

"Just a minute, Bill." The sound of his name made him

stop and look at her. She went on hesitantly: "If it really means so much to you and your friends, having someone on that fourth quarter . . . and if the others are willing to accept me . . . then I'll ride the dun mare, and I promise to set my stake where you tell me. It's the least I could do."

Emery's dark face broke into a slow grin. "Why, that's fine!" he exclaimed. "That's dandy! Let's go talk to the boys."

II

Full dark had descended over the prairie now, but it brought no rest and no quiet. The thousands jammed along the periphery of the Cherokee Strip, waiting with febrile impatience for the passing of this last night and the dawning of the long-awaited day, would know little rest before morning. There was a constant seething—a galloping of horses along the line, a calling of voices, not infrequently the sharp rattle of guns. When shooting was heard, the ugly, muttered comment—"One less!"—generally followed.

Bill and Laura walked among the campfires that dotted the plain, like stars dropped from the deepening sky overhead; they passed the wagon camps, and listened to the voices that held a mutual, high-keyed tension. Once, Laura gasped and caught Bill's hand, pointed to the south into the dark immensity of the Strip that lay, vast and empty, beyond the deadline. "What's that?" she cried. "That glow against the sky?"

"Grass fire," he murmured. "I've heard the military has been burning off the bunch grass . . . some say to smoke out the Sooners, others that it's to make the surveyor's markers easier to find. I dunno. I hope the old Figure Eight doesn't catch and burn, before we have a chance to claim it."

They found Mac and Ed Coulton seated by their fire. They looked at the girl with Bill and came stumbling to their feet, old Mac exclaiming: "What . . . what you got here, Bill?"

The latter made introductions, and, from the looks that his friends gave Laura Cain, he wondered for the first time if he had made a mistake. But he went ahead to tell them of the girl's plight, and of the suggested loan of a horse, in return for her aid in securing the Figure 8. The silence that followed was so prolonged that he turned acutely embarrassed and began to wish for the girl's sake that he had never brought her into this.

"All right," he said angrily. "If you don't like the idea, you could at least say so. Maybe you don't care what happens to our plans . . . but you don't have to just stand there staring."

McIvor said quickly: "I'm sorry. I was just thinking." He turned to the girl. "If, as you say, you don't want to get permanently mixed up in a town company, we could probably buy you out in a few months. I was in the Civil War, so I can exercise my veteran's rights and get immediate title to my land after a year's residence, and borrow enough on it to pay yours out, too. And, believe me, there'll be plenty of claims going begging by then . . . after the first hard winter has cleaned some of the danged fools off them. You'll be able to buy any farm land you want cheap . . . and with cash left over to hire men to do the heavy work for you. That sound like a fair bargain?"

"It does," Laura Cain agreed. Her eyes were suspiciously bright in the firelight. "I . . . I don't know what to say."

A sound from Ed Coulton brought Bill's glance to him. Ed's bony face was dark and scowling; his long jaw shot forward. At Bill's challenging look, the other man shrugged and suddenly turned and strode away to stand staring out into the darkness at the scattered campfires.

He certainly looked as though he disapproved of what had been decided, but, since he chose to say nothing, Bill Emery decided to pay no attention to him. He told the girl: "It's settled, then. I'll dig up a saddle for the mare and bring her around to your camp in the morning. You sure you'll be safe, alone?"

"I can take care of myself," she assured him. "I keep a gun in the wagon."

They talked a little longer, and then she left them to return to her own camp. Watching her move away into the fire-lit darkness, Bill was troubled with the thought of her being here, in all the confusion and wildness of the impending run—with no man for protection, not even the companionship of another woman. But just now there was something else that demanded ironing out. He turned, and sought Ed Coulton's attention. He said: "You don't like this arrangement?"

Ed walked back to the fire; the hard set of his jaw made dark hollows in his gaunt cheeks. "Am I supposed to like the idea of you pickin' up some honky-tonker and . . . ?"

Bill hit him, a single hard blow, that splatted sharply against the side of Ed Coulton's jaw. Ed went, sprawling, into the dust. There was a cry from McIvor and the old cowpuncher got to Bill and grabbed his arm. "Damn it, boy!" he exclaimed. "No!"

Standing over his friend, Bill felt the quick gnawing of regret. The blow had been undesigned—a harsh, instinctive thing. Yet hadn't he had an idea similar to Coulton's, in the moment when he met Laura Cain?

He shook off Mac's hand, but made no other movement. Ed Coulton was fingering his jaw, shocked anger in his stare. Slowly he picked himself up from the ground, stood facing Emery. "All right," he muttered. "Maybe I shouldn't've said it. But I sure as the devil know what I *think!*"

"Then think it. But keep it to yourself!"

"Well, if both of you have made up your minds, I reckon I'm outvoted and there's nothin' I can say."

Old Mac, the peacemaker, said: "After all, Ed, she don't look like one of them kind of women."

"You believe that windy about losing her horses?" Ed lashed back. "Looks like Bill sure swallowed it!"

35

Emery's fists curled tightly again, despite himself. "You never heard her . . . you never seen her crying. You'd have believed her, too."

The other made a gesture, palms flung wide. "Go ahead, then! It's your bronc' she talked you out of. Just don't start handin' out anything that belongs to *me!*" He had started to turn away; he swung back. "And I just want to tell you this. I've seen that girl somewhere. I ain't placed her yet, but I blamed sure mean to."

"All right," Bill gritted. "Tell us about it when you do." He was breathing hard, trying to keep control of himself, trying to remember that Ed Coulton had been his saddle partner for a long, long time, and that it wasn't right that they should fuss now over a thing like this.

McIvor drifted to his side, a frown on his face as they watched Ed stride off into the dark. "Ed's a suspicious one," old Mac opined. "You know how prone he is to get ringy about a deal he can't see all the angles to. It's admittedly a poor way for him to talk about a girl as nice as this Laurie Cain stacks up, but . . . well, he's worried, and he's got a right to his say."

"Yeah," Bill said, and shrugged. "So we'll forget it."

"And sleep on it. Ed will probably feel differently, come morning."

But the scene had built a strange barrier among these friends that words could not break down. There wasn't much said, as the hours dragged out. Even garrulous Mac soon gave up attempting to restore the old congenial atmosphere and, getting out his clasp knife, busied himself with pointing up a length of hickory that, with a crude flag tied to it, would serve tomorrow to stake his claim. Bill looked to his horses, then, without a word to the others, walked away from their camp.

Laura Cain had said she would make out all right alone;

still, he couldn't help a feeling of uneasiness about her. He would take a look to make sure everything was all right with her. If it looked to be so, he'd not bother the girl, but he'd feel better in his own mind.

Then, only yards from Laura Cain's wagon camp, he hauled to a sudden stop.

Between him and the fire, two silhouettes shaped up against its cherry glow. One was the small, round-breasted figure of the girl, the other that of a tall, solid-built man whose profile appeared strong and virile. They were talking urgently—arguing perhaps. Bill Emery, uncertain whether to stay or walk away, saw Laura shake her head, saw the man take her by her shoulder. She shook her head again, lifted a hand against his chest as though she would push him from her.

With a sudden movement, the man swept her, still protesting, into his arms. Bill took a step forward—and then, in the firelight, saw the gleam of the girl's own white arms creeping up about the man's broad shoulders. Her struggles ceased, and the two stood there, melted in a tight embrace.

Silently Bill Emery turned and faded into the shadows. There was a hollow place somewhere within him, although he told himself there was no reason why he should have this gnawing of disappointment. What did he know, after all, about Laura Cain? As he stumbled back through the darkness to his own camp, Ed Coulton's words kept beating through his mind.

He still couldn't believe that all the things Ed had hinted at were true, although there was no good reason why he shouldn't. His mouth hardened, twisted cynically. No need to waste his time worrying about Laura Cain—apparently alone and friendless in the night. It looked as though she had taken settlement of that problem into her own hands.

"Oh, the devil with it," he muttered.

III

Morning—the morning of September 16th, 1893—dawned clear and cloudless, with nothing to break the merciless oven blast of the sun in a brassy sky. A fierce hot wind came sweeping across the Strip, blowing the scorched scent of fire-blackened prairie to the thousands who crowded along the Kansas border. This was the day at last that they had all been awaiting with feverish impatience since the President's proclamation a month earlier. And the whole 180-mile line seethed with last hurried preparations as noon dragged slowly nearer.

Old McIvor, bitten by the fever of excitement, could hardly keep still or hold himself to the last-minute chores that had to be done, but a reserve still held between Bill and Ed Coulton and made them both strangely silent. Ed's jaw was swollen and discolored; sight of the bruise served to remind Emery of the night before and, coupled with Ed's surly manner, made speech between them difficult.

Bill Emery himself was not in any mood for talking. He busied himself with a thorough, final check of his gear—hunting for any weak places in the saddle harness that might need strengthening with twists of haywire. He had a wild, hard ride ahead of him over treacherous ground; any spill or break could mean death, under such conditions. Fortunately both the piebald gelding and the little dun mare were sure-footed saddle broncos, long on speed and well bottomed for endurance. There wouldn't be anyone better mounted in the race.

He had just finished with checking the shoeing job on both animals, when Laura Cain walked into the camp. Bill straightened slowly, setting down the mare's hoof. He had not looked forward to her coming, knowing it wasn't going to be easy to talk to her while in his mind he would be seeing the thing he had stumbled across the night before. He had not even been certain that she would show up again. But whoever the man was that had made love to her by the campfire, she came and she came alone, and perhaps he only imagined that there was a subdued, troubled unhappiness about her. The smile she gave him seemed warm enough.

Bill didn't bother to return the smile; there was naked, unreasoning jealousy in him and he knew it, although he recognized that he was foolish to let himself be bothered by its stabbing prod. McIvor, seeing nothing wrong here, hobbled over to greet Laura.

"You all set to race the field for a hundred sixty acres of Cherokee land?" He offered her a sharpened stick of hickory wood. "Here . . . I whittled this out for you. You'll need somep'n for a flag . . . cloth of some kind."

She smiled, thanking him. "I've got an old petticoat I can tear up." She was dressed sensibly for the ride ahead of her in a blouse and divided skirt and half boots, and a flat-topped hat with a rawhide throat latch.

Bill told her: "We'll have to cache your wagon and everything else you can spare, and come back for them afterwards. Main thing is to travel light. We'll have to carry food and water. It's been a dry season, and I doubt there's a creek running in the Strip . . . even Cherry Creek has gone dry, so we'll have to take shovels and put a well down, first thing. This is the bronc' I spoke about." He gave the dun mare a slap on the shoulder. "She's sure-footed and as easy as a rocking chair."

"She's a beauty!" Laura exclaimed. "Thank you again for letting me ride her."

Past the girl's dark head, Bill caught a sour look on the face of Ed Coulton. His own manner as he said—"It's all right!"—was so curt that she stared at him with troubled eyes. He turned away, not meeting them.

It was only minutes now. The hands of the old silver watch that McIvor hauled from his pocket for a hundredth time within the past half hour were scissoring down on the figure twelve at the top of the dial. And suddenly, as at a signal, a suffocating weight of silence spread across the lineup of stampeders, massed tightly against the invisible boundary and waiting in tense breathlessness for the signal.

The four of them had managed, with considerable maneuvering, to work their horses into the very front of the throng. On either hand, it stretched off beyond the horizon to east and west; at their backs were other horsemen, and, behind these, various types of light buggies and rigs, with the farm wagons and big prairie schooners crowded to the rear. Silent under a broiling sky, every person had eyes set on the empty prairie ahead, and on the thin line of blue-clad foot soldiers that stood facing them with rifles at the ready.

A mile or so eastward, on the Rock Island tracks, an engine waited with steam up and a string of cattle cars loaded to the roof with boomers. According to the rules, the engineer was expected to hold the throttle down to a speed no greater than that of a running horse in order that the train's passengers should have no advantage over the rest of the land seekers, but Ed Coulton, with his usual cynicism, had voiced the opinion that enough $10 bills thrust under the trainman's nose would suffice to make that regulation a dead letter.

Any horsebacker who expected to stake a claim within a quarter mile of the tracks, anywhere along the line, would undoubtedly find them all taken by men from the cattle cars, regardless of the fact that these were supposed to be headed only for various town sites that had been laid out along the right of way. "Damned bunch of legal Sooners," Ed summed it up sourly.

Suddenly Bill told the girl at his stirrup: "Look sharp!"

The soldiers out front had raised their rifles to shoulders, were squinting along the bright barrels toward the brassy sky. The mass of land seekers strained forward, like a great animal waiting for the leash to be slipped.

Then, rolling down the line in a crackling of rifles, the signal passed quickly across their front. With a mighty roar the line broke, and a tide of horses and riders and rigs boiled and flooded into the Cherokee Strip.

Yipping shrilly in his own excitement, Bill kicked his pony with the spurs and lifted it ahead into a dead run that put it well into the forefront of that yelling mob, and Ed and Mac were hard abreast of him. There was Laura, however, and a backward glance warned him that she was having trouble. The sudden, thunderous confusion—and a strange rider up—had unsettled the dun mare so that it shied, and a second bronco roaring past dealt the horse a hard shouldering blow that started it circling.

Cursing under his breath, Bill pulled back. With the ground shaking underneath to the mad thudding of hoofs, and dust and grit swirling about them in a fog, he reached and grabbed the mare's bridle, helped Laura get straightened out. He caught a glimpse of her face, pale with fear. "Come on!" he shouted. "Stick close to me!"

They surged ahead, stirrup to stirrup now. Their place at the head of the wave had long since been lost, and Mac and Ed were gone from sight. Neither of these facts concerned him too greatly.

He was gambling on his sure knowledge of the country to give him the advantage and make up for any loss of time. He spurred on, through the heat and the fog of hoof-raised dust that drifted, red and choking, all about them and cut down the field of vision. Laura, sticking closely at his side, was proving now that she could handle a horse with considerable skill.

They had lost so much time that the first wave of riders had passed them, and even some of the quickest light rigs went spinning by. But it was only a matter of seconds before they overtook these, once they got their horses running steadily. As they pulled even with a pair of the rigs, it was to see one of them swerve as it struck a buried rock—tilt onto two wheels, right itself, and then swing crashing into the other wagon. Both smashed up in a tangle of harness and horses and spinning wheels. Bill Emery heard a choked cry break from Laura and turned to her. "Don't stop!" he shouted.

This was every man for himself. You didn't pause, no matter what you saw happen.

The ground lifted, fell away as they crested a rise, and shot down across a patch of burned-over land. Fire still smoldered in the roots of the grasses, and the earth steamed and smoked, and stubble crackled under their horses' hoofs, throwing back a stench of charred weeds. They crossed this, eyes stung to tears by the smoke and the flung ashes.

Now Bill was pulling his gelding toward the right, shouldering Laura's mount gradually in that direction. The smoke cleared; they hit the edge of the burn, and a dry watercourse lined with drought-seared elms angled between a pair of rounded hills. Bill pointed into it, and sand and gravel yielded underfoot as they dropped into this gully.

On they galloped, the rounded hills lifting higher. The other riders seemed to have by-passed this twisting gully. They were alone, the roar of many hoofs for the moment fallen away; in the comparative quiet, there was only the slapping echoes of their own broncos clattering over rounded creek pebbles.

From somewhere came a sound of gunfire that ceased and began again and abruptly fell away. Laura threw a questioning look at Bill Emery and his mouth took on a hard grin. "Somebody just settled a little argument over a claim!" he shouted. "It's starting already! And there'll be plenty more to come!"

They broke out of the gully into a wedge of grassland that fell away gently toward a bottom, and then lifted again to meet the pale horizon dead ahead. Far over eastward, they glimpsed a flank of the rushing mob pouring into the hollow and across the rise, but the stretch in front of them lay open and empty except for the tawny streak of a coyote, frightened and scurrying across country with tail between his legs.

Halfway to the bottom, Bill heard Laura's scream. He looked around in time to see the horse go plummeting under her in a rolling fall.

It took him only seconds to pull the gelding to a sliding halt and turn back, throwing reins as he leaped from saddle. The mare was already lurching to its feet, but the girl lay where she had fallen. Bill ran to her on legs that were suddenly weak and unsteady. Laura was on her back, eyes closed, her face very pale against the dark hair that a ground breeze blew against it. But when he dropped to his knees beside her, he saw with infinite relief that her breast, inside the white blouse, was lifting and falling regularly.

"Laura!" he heard his own voice crying hoarsely, as he took her hand and began to chafe it. "Baby. . . ."

He had thought to bring a canteen from his saddle, and, hastily wetting a corner of his neck cloth, he bathed her face. At the touch of the water, the girl's breathing quickened, her eyelids stirred. Bill eased an arm below her shoulders, lifted her against a knee, and placed the canteen to her lips.

She gagged at first, then, reviving, managed to swallow a little. She opened her eyes, looked about her a little blankly before understanding returned.

"You took a spill," Bill Emery explained quickly, seeing her bewilderment. "Reckon you broke anything?"

"I'll . . . let you know in a minute," she said, her voice shaky. She looked around. "The horse?"

"She's all right." He was oddly pleased that she should have thought first of the mare. "You just rest here a minute until you're sure you feel strong enough."

But memory flooded her eyes, and Laura Cain shook her head anxiously. "We're losing time!" she cried. "We've got to go on. . . ."

He would have detained her but she was determined, and he helped her to rise, one arm still about her shoulders. He had to clutch her tightly and hold her like that for a moment as a brief spell of dizziness passed. Laura shook her head to clear it, brushed back the dark hair from her forehead. "I'm fine now," she said. "Really!" He released her, and stooped to pick up his canteen and sling it across a shoulder.

The dun mare, however, was lame. This was a shocking discovery. Bill Emery hastily examined the injured leg, while the horse turned its head to watch what he was doing. "Nothing serious," Bill decided. "It'll work that limp out. But we've got to ride double from here on. It's not too far. The gelding can make it."

Laura showed real distress, despite his assurances. "I'm awfully sorry," she said. "Honestly I am."

"Nothing you could have helped," he grunted. He turned to the gelding, held the stirrup for her to mount. "Quick, now. Take the saddle. I'll stick on behind."

They rode on, with the lame mare following on lead reins,

and Bill Emery's arms about the girl, guiding the piebald. With her soft body so close against him, and the strong wind blowing her hair about his face, Laura's presence was troubling. He remembered the stab of terror that had struck through him at seeing her lying motionlessly on the earth after the accident. He recalled, only now, the tender foolishness he had babbled as he knelt chafing her wrists. He thought: *You blamed idiot! Even after last night?*

But some things can't be helped. It seemed very much as though—in spite of anything he could do about it—he was falling in love with this girl of whom he really knew nothing at all except that he had seen her in the passionate embrace of another man.

They rode on, Bill holding the gelding to a long, reaching gait that it could maintain without tiring too badly, even with an extra rider up. They went into a brief stretch of rough country, the red soil broken by outcroppings of sandstone, and skirted a knot of pecan trees where wild turkeys, roosting in the branches, took off and went flapping through the tall grass as they pounded by. They had seen no other riders for some minutes. Now a sound reached them that made the girl turn her head: "More gunfire . . . straight ahead of us."

Bill nodded bleakly. "I hear it. And Figure Eight is just across that next rise."

He lifted the gelding with a stab of steel; they went up the rise on a new burst of speed.

The fires had not reached this place. Sod-roofed ranch buildings stood in a weed-grown yard, below a slope of tawny, sun-cured buffalo grass, with the dried-out course of Cherry Creek winding beyond. The main house, the bunkshack dug-out, and barns were crudely but substantially built. In the corral, a half dozen horses ran about, frightened by the blast of guns.

Bill Emery had quickly reined in, and the gun from his belt holster was in his fingers and his face had gone rock hard at what he saw and heard in the quiet afternoon. The rattle of gunfire came from the house, from the other buildings—the guns hidden, their whereabouts told only by the wisps of powder smoke that lifted and filmed at windows and doors only opened a crack, their owners keeping carefully out of · sight.

In the open, in the dirt of the hard-packed ranch yard, a single figure was visible. It lay motionless, face down, with arms and legs thrown in a grotesque sprawl. The ground wind plucked at the white hair of McIvor's stilled head, and at the bit of cloth beneath his outstretched hand—the flour sack flag tied to the stake that he'd whittled out for the purpose of claiming his land.

In a shallow swale, between this ridge and the ranch buildings, Ed Coulton had apparently managed to find cover of a sort. Bill could see him crouched there. Even as he looked, Ed raised up to throw a bullet toward the ranch house, and then ducked into his narrow shelter again.

"Here," grunted Bill, and stuffed the reins into Laura's hands and slid quickly across the gelding's rump. "They ran into trouble. Sooners, it looks like. Ain't a chance that anybody could have made the run and got here ahead of Mac and Ed. You stay here, and look out for your own skin. If they should get the best of us, and start after you, don't hesitate a minute to take the gelding and ride for it. You understand?"

He didn't wait to hear Laura's answer, but was already going forward down the slope at a bent run. He thought he caught the girl's voice, calling after him, calling his name— "Bill . . . wait!"—but he would not look back.

Six-gun ready, he went down that slope in a hurried, weaving course. At the house, guns had quickly discovered

46

him and were reaching with leaden fingers. There were rifles in that crowd of ambushers, which made it bad for an enemy armed only with a handgun, all that he or Ed Coulton could bring to this fight. Bill heard the shriek of a slug with the drive of a Winchester behind it as it sliced the air too close to him. But he kept moving, and the buildings grew larger and so did the still, motionless shape of old Mac who had been his friend.

Then Ed Coulton was in front of him, turning and rising from his hiding place to wave Bill in with a smoking gun barrel. Moments later, Bill Emery dived into the protection of the hollow, beside the other man, just beating out a bullet that might have drilled his skull.

Ed's gaunt face was shiny with sweat and dirt-streaked. There was the beginning of panic in his eyes, and a burning hatred. "Damn them!" he gritted over and over, between chattering teeth. "Damn them!"

"Got any idea who they are?" Bill demanded. "Or how many?"

The other shook his head. "They was waitin' for us . . . all staked out with their guns ready when we came into the yard unsuspectin' until we sighted them bronc's in the corral. By then it was too late. The first volley got Mac." His head shook, mouth warped by bitterness. "Damned Sooners! Look at those horses . . . not a drop of sweat on any of 'em. That's proof enough, I reckon, of how the skunks managed to get here ahead of us!"

In a sudden access of fury, he lifted his gun toward the corral, but Bill put a hand on the barrel, struck it down. "You don't mean that, Ed," he pointed out calmly. "Killin' the horses won't get us anything. Save your lead for their owners."

At the same moment, a flit of movement across the yard

brought his head around and his own six-gun leaped upward. A man had broken suddenly from the bunkshack doorway and was making a running dash for a small tack shed a dozen yards away. Jaw set, Bill swung down on him and made a hasty shot, but he hadn't time to aim and the slug went wide. Before he could shoot again, the Sooner had gained the doorway.

Ed cursed. "I was afraid somebody would think of that. Watch the window. From there, he's got an angle to pick us right out of this hole."

The window had a wooden covering, hinged to swing out from the tack shed wall. Even as Ed spoke, Bill saw it move. It swung wide, propelled by the snout of a rifle shoved across the sill—the man was being very careful not to expose himself. Bill Emery's fist tightened on the six-gun, but he had no target, and it was plain that Ed had called the deal correctly. Cramped in this shallow hole, they would be sitting ducks for the rifleman at the shed window.

"Let's get out of here," grunted Emery.

He slammed a wild shot in the direction of the shed window, for whatever good it might do in holding the rifleman off his target, then he was pushing Ed to his feet, and lunging after him.

Their goal was a corner of the hay barn, but they never made it. The distance was just too great, the fury of lead that the forted-up guns threw at them too terrible. Emery stumbled to the burn of a slug across his thigh that missed, by a fraction of timing, crippling him for good. Ahead of him he saw Ed Coulton's hat lifted from his head and sent rolling. Next instant, they both dived for the ground and for the concealment of the tall weeds that were dry and dead and brittle.

Bill hugged the ground, panting, with teeth set against the pain of his bullet-swiped leg. There was no cover here. A few rounds lacing the brittle stalks should suffice to finish this job and leave him and Ed as limp and still as poor old McIvor out there in the open yard.

To his astonishment, however, the shooting had all at once halted. There was a sudden, breathless silence, broken only by the humming of insects in the weeds close to his face, and the shallow rasp of his own breathing. Then a voice sounded across the silence—a hard, confident voice, speaking from over in the direction of the main house.

"Emery! Coulton! You hear me?"

Bill caught his breath, and looked at Ed who had turned to stare at him.

"Who the hell is it?" Coulton whispered hoarsely. "That voice sounds familiar."

"Not to me," grunted Bill. "But he knows our names, whoever it is."

"You two had better listen hard!" the voice came again, pitched louder. "It's your last chance to be reasonable. Throw down your guns and walk toward us, or we'll rake those weeds with lead and cut you both in two! Which is it going to be? You got just five minutes to decide!"

The silence dropped again, and the buzzing of gnats became startlingly loud in the ears of the men trapped in the weeds. Bill Emery hitched forward, careful not to show himself. With the sharp ends of broken weed stalks raking him and their dry dust working into his nostrils and under his clothing, he wriggled up beside his friend and said harshly: "What do we do now?"

"Ain't a thing we can do," Ed Coulton answered between his teeth. "We make a break for it, and they'll tear us apart with those damned rifles. We surrender, and they'll kill us anyhow."

Emery poked his gun barrel into the growth that fronted his face, separating it for a look at the silent ranch yard.

Except for Mac's body, unmoving under the heavy smash of the sun, and the stir of the corralled horses, nothing showed. But within the house, the voice bawled again: "Time's running out! You decided yet?"

"Getting anxious," Emery grunted. "He don't know how soon another bunch may come riding in here, and he wants us out of the way before they do."

Coulton shook his head. "Why can't I remember that voice? I know it, all right. I've heard it before somewhere, and not too long ago. It's no accident, either, them knowing our names like that."

About to answer, Bill Emery turned, startled by a crackling in the dry growth at his back. He stared in consternation. "Laura!" he cried. "Go back! Do you hear me?"

She came straight on, crawling on hands and knees. The sweat that Bill could feel streaming on his face and hands was not entirely due, just then, to the suffocating pressure of weed-trapped heat. As the girl dropped down beside him, he shook his head with a groan of despair. "Why did you do such a fool thing as this? Ain't you got any better sense?"

Her face looked white. "Bill." She placed a hand on his arm and he could feel it trembling—thought there was a note of pleading in her voice. But then her mouth tightened, with a set of determination in it.

Before he could fathom what she was about to do, she slid her hand down his arm and deftly plucked the gun from his fingers. The round bore of the weapon swung to cover both men. "Don't move!" she cried hoarsely. "You drop your gun, Mister Coulton!"

Stunned, Bill heard Ed's grunt of surprise, his muffled oath. "What double-cross is this?"

"You heard what I said," Laura told him. "Throw your gun away."

After a moment, there came the sound of crackling weeds, the *thud* of the weapon into the dirt as Ed Coulton reluctantly obeyed the order and the authority of the leveled gun. At the same instant came the voice from the main house in a final warning: "All right, you two! Time's up! You had your chance. . . ."

"Wait, Morgan!" cried Laura. "They're coming out with their hands up. Don't shoot!"

"Morgan!" Ed Coulton echoed. "Morgan Banning . . . that's who it is! And you. . . ." He cursed. "I told you last night I'd seen her before, Bill."

A leaden weight seemed to have solidified within Bill Emery. His stare heavy on Laura Cain's white face, he asked dully: "Who is she, then?"

"She's Banning's woman. Her real name is Belle Conway. She's a singer and come-on girl in that Dodge City clip joint of his. You satisfied now with what you've went and done to us?"

Before the steady beat of Emery's bitter gaze, the girl's own eyes wavered. Her face was entirely without color. But then her breast lifted with resolution and she said firmly: "Get on your feet."

There was no choice. Grim of face, the two captives crawled out into the open. With the girl at their backs, and that leveled gun covering them, they moved toward the men who were already pouring out of the ranch buildings with saddle guns and revolvers in their hands.

Bill saw the one he knew must be Morgan Banning—recognized the solid build of him, the handsome features now twisted in a grin of triumph. He had seen him once before—last night, silhouetted against the dancing glow of a campfire, with Laura Cain locked tightly in his embrace.

IV

"Three kid sisters," Ed Coulton was muttering bitterly from the corner of his mouth. "Boy, what a line she sold you. Morgan had her posted looking for suckers . . . and, when she found you, she knew she'd got him the real prize, all right."

Emery couldn't say anything. He had had plenty of warning; he had even seen the girl and Banning together, when—he knew now—she must have been passing on to her man all she had learned about Figure 8 and its special possibilities. Yet, he had let a pretty face and a clever act fool him and dull his caution. Even now he could hardly convince himself that the girl was what she was, and not what she had pretended to be.

But there could be little doubting the possessive gleam in Morgan Banning's eyes as he looked at the girl, nodding and smiling, and told her: "Good work, Belle. I'm not sure this pair of fools would have had the sense to give in without making us waste a lot of lead knocking them out of that weed patch." He jerked his head at a couple of the men with him. "Griffen! Duke! Take charge of them . . . and watch out for tricks."

One of the pair stepped forward and did a quick job of frisking the prisoners. With their guns removed, all that either of them carried in the way of a weapon was Bill Emery's clasp knife, and this was taken from him.

They were a hard-looking bunch of men that Banning commanded—men with the clear mark of killers and hired gunfighters. Three of them had followed their boss into the open. While Griffen and Duke took care of the prisoners the girl had brought in, the third gunman walked over to

52

McIvor's body and turned it over upon its back, revealing the smear of blood on the oldster's forehead and on the ground where it had lain. He picked up the six-gun that had slid partly from its holster when old Mac fell.

Suddenly he straightened, turning to call to Banning. "Hey! There's still some life in this one!"

The saloon owner had an arm possessively around the girl's waist. He grunted: "The hell you say. Well, Duke will help you get him out of sight. Put him in the bunkshack . . . and this pair with him. Quick! I hear riders."

In fact, the drum of hoofs could be heard now, swelling above the ridge to the north. Feverish activity seized the men in the ranch yard. The one named Duke ran to help lift old Mac's limp body; Griffen shoved a gun barrel into Bill Emery's middle. "Move," he commanded.

Even with the approach of possible help, there was no hope in stalling. Shrugging resignedly, the prisoners let themselves be prodded in the direction of the shack.

Like many such constructions in the dry plains country, this was a dug-out—built of mud and logs, above a hole sunk some half dozen feet into the ground. Steps, chopped in the earth, led down into the dark interior, the floor was the hard-trodden dirt, and the furnishings consisted of a double tier of bunks ranged around the crude walls and a rough deal table and benches.

It had nothing elegant about it, but Bill Emery had lived here for a couple of years and had learned that a dug-out could be more comfortable—cooler in summer, warmer in winter—than more ambitious dwellings.

McIvor having been toted in and deposited carelessly on one of the bunks, the other two were ordered in after him, and the door, of heavy planking, was dropped into place across the opening. It didn't fit too well, letting a streak of daylight enter through a wide crack between the top of the door and the roof, and, with the aid of this faint illumination, Bill Emery groped his way to the bunk where Mac's colored shirt showed faintly in the gloom.

Anxiously he felt for a pulse; it was there, faint but steady, and the old cowpuncher's breathing sounded normal. The bullet had evidently creased his skull, and maybe it was nothing worse than that.

Meanwhile, approaching horsemen were upon the ranch. Ed hauled a bench over to the door and stood on it, to put his eye to the crack where light streamed in. "Can you see anything?" Bill asked him.

"Not much."

A shout reached them—Morgan Banning's harsh voice, lifted in warning. "Ride on! All this land hereabout has been claimed!"

One of the newcomers said something—a challenge plainly, for Banning's rejoinder held an angry threat. "I said, these claims are taken! You got eyes? You see them stakes? Anybody dares touch them is askin' for a bellyful of lead! Now, beat it!"

A moment's silence—then, the horses were in motion again. They could tell that the riders, bluffed out, were swinging wide; the clattering of shoe irons on loose pebbles sounded as they rattled across the dry course of Cherry Creek. The sounds quickly faded.

They had scarcely gone from hearing when more riders came racing across the hill after them. The flood of the run had at last hit this place with full force, and now for a period of twenty minutes or so Morgan Banning's men had their hands full, meeting and turning it aside. Some of the stampeders wanted to argue; most gave way to the threat of guns, and went on fast. But once, there were harsh words that gave way abruptly to a rattle of gunfire.

Ed Coulton, thinking he saw in this a diversion that would give him his opportunity, at once attacked the door and pushed it away from the opening, wide enough to slip through. Bill, seeing what he was up to, called sharply—"Watch yourself!"—and started across the room after him. At that instant a high-powered rifle bullet struck the dug-out entrance, ricocheted angrily away, and dumped a shower of dirt upon them both. Ed yelped and ducked inside again, stumbling into his companion.

Plainly Banning's men weren't being caught off guard. Somebody had been given orders to keep an eye on the dugout, and there was no use trying to break out of it.

Now the last wave of horsebackers had hit the Figure 8, and here came the wheeled rigs, the light buckboards, after them the slower-moving farm wagons, and finally the grotesquely lumbering prairie schooners. The men in these wagons held even less fight than the horsemen who had come before. They rode right by, not stopping to argue or question the authority of the gunmen who held the ranch buildings. Eventually the tide thinned, and the last disheartened stragglers passed. Thus the run swept over this part of the Strip, and the sound of hoofs and wheels ended and dust they had thrown up drifted and settled. Silence came back upon the Figure 8 headquarters.

A crunching of boots sounded outside the bunkshack; the plank door was lifted away, and Morgan Banning came down the steps into the gloom of the place. The girl, and one of his gunmen, accompanied him. To the latter, Banning growled: "Strike a light!"

A lantern hung on the wall and this was set burning, its yellow glow washing aside the shadows and glinting on the guns Banning and the other carried.

Banning jerked his head at the girl. "Go ahead, if you insist, Belle, and do what you want to with the old guy over there." The girl Emery had known as Laura Cain nodded and, without looking at the men she had betrayed, brushed past them and went to McIvor's bunk. She looked at the bloody furrow across his scalp and said: "I'll need water."

At a nod from Banning, his henchman passed over to her the canteen he had brought, slung over his shoulder. There was a ripping of cloth as Belle Conway tore a strip from the hem of her underskirt; wetting it, she began to work washing the blood from McIvor's head.

"Don't waste too much time on him," Banning commented. "We got a ride to make, and afternoon's wearing out. Got to get down to Enid, to record these claims, and send off a wire for supplies."

Ed Coulton couldn't hold himself in any longer. "Dirty stinkin' Sooners . . . !"

Banning's knuckles came up and batted him, open-handed, across the mouth. Ed staggered a little, caught himself; the gun in Banning's fist checked his angry rush. The saloon owner showed strong, white teeth in a grin.

"Duke," he told his man, "I'm leavin' you and Griffen in charge of things. Don't take nothing off these monkeys, nothing at all. Better start them digging a well, or we're apt to get pretty dry when our water gives out." He lifted a sleeve, ran it across his sweaty face. "Damn this heat!"

The man called Duke had listened to his orders sullenly. "OK, Morgan," he grunted.

"After that," Banning went on, "we'll be ready to go ahead. We'll incorporate, get our town site registered, and start peddling real estate. It's a sweet set-up." He grinned at his captives. "I got to hand it to you guys for seeing the possibilities. I wasn't sure but what it might be a crackpot idea, until I had a look for myself. But it's obvious there ain't a more natural spot for a town in the whole Strip. And it'll be Morgan Banning's town . . . all of it. Then, one day, when a railroad follows that freight trail in. . . ."

Bill Emery couldn't keep the stinging bitterness from his voice. "Betrayal pays big dividends, I guess. Just watch out that someone doesn't turn the same trick against you sometime, Banning."

"It won't do them any good," the saloon owner said easily. "There's some that have tried it and found the going a little too rough for them." He had been seated on the corner of the table as they talked; now he swung to his feet, telling the girl sharply: "Come along, Belle. You've taken enough time with that."

She said: "One minute."

Once her job was finished, she gathered up the canteen and scraps of cloth and walked straight past Bill Emery, her shoulders stiff, her eyes without expression and fixed straight in front of her, She went through the doorway and up the dug-out steps into the sunlight. In the bunk, old Mac lay still unconscious, but with the blood gone from his whiskered face and clean white bandage fashioned about his head.

Banning gave his prisoners a last, satisfied look. "Make yourselves comfortable till I get back. Ain't made up my mind yet what I'm gonna do with the three of you."

"I can tell you what you *better* do with us," Ed Coulton told him harshly. "Especially if McIvor should happen to die from that head wound."

The man did not bother to answer. He turned his broad back and went up the steps, sheathing his gun. The gunslinger called Duke followed him, but moving backward and with his weapon ready and leveled. The door was not put into place again; it had no bar or any way to fasten it, and

Banning's men knew their prisoners would not be foolish enough to ask for murder by trying to make a break up that narrow dug-out entrance.

"And that's that!" growled Ed Coulton.

Emery didn't answer. Instead, he walked over to look at the bandage the girl had put on old Mac. She had done a good job, and there didn't seem to be any fresh bleeding. But the oldster's continued lack of consciousness bothered him. He felt helpless in the face of it.

Presently horses were saddled and brought from the corral to the house—five of them. They couldn't see the door of the house from their prison, but when a body of riders broke from the ranch yard, heading for the dry crossing of Cherry Creek, they watched them out of sight. Morgan Banning and the girl headed them. Of the other three, one they had seen earlier and a second had something strangely familiar about the way he filled the saddle. They had vanished in the willows lining the dry creek before Emery could figure out what it might be.

That left behind only a pair of guards, Duke and Griffen, to watch the prisoners. However, without weapons, the latter had small chance against two armed and careful enemies. They could only sit in the gloom of the dug-out, listening to old Mac's quiet breathing and feeling the sweat run off their bodies, and the parched thirst that heat put in their throats.

"All right, you two!" a voice called finally—a voice they recognized as belonging to the man named Duke. "Come out of there. We got a little chore for you!"

They exchanged a look, rose, and climbed the steps into the open, squinting as the dazzle of afternoon struck their eyes.

Outside, they found Banning's men waiting with ready guns, and at Griffen's feet lay a couple of spades. Bill Emery knew the purpose for which they had been summoned from their prison; a faint stirring of hope began within him. A spade was a poor weapon against a gun, and yet. . . .

"What about the old boy?" Griffen asked dubiously.

"I'll take a look," said Duke, and disappeared into the bunkshack. He came out a minute later. "Not a sign of rousing. Leave him be." He jerked his head at Emery, and pointed to the spades. "Pick them up, and start walking. We'll tell you when to stop."

Without a word, Emery stepped and shouldered the tools.

Griffen asked his partner: "Where'll we take 'em?"

"Creekbed's as sure a place as any."

"OK. Head out."

They shuffled through the dry red dust, the prisoners walking ahead, the guards following with a gun and a rifle covering them. Cherry Creek, generally a never-failing stream, had dried out in this severe period of drought until it was no more than a sandy-bottomed trough, lined with boulders and sere, yellow-leafed cottonwoods and willows. They clambered down into the dry bed. Griffen looked around, then picked a spot and marked it with his heel.

"There," he said. "Morgan wants a well . . . and we're gonna let you dig it for him. We're bein' easy on you, too. Nice soft sand to work in, and probably no distance to speak of down to the water table. Get busy!"

He turned on his heel and walked over to join Duke, who had already seated himself against the bank in the tree shade. Plainly enough they had chosen this place less out of consideration for the prisoners than for their own convenience. It gave them a shady place where they could rest in comfort while they watched the labors of the well diggers. Emery and Coulton exchanged a glance and thrust their spades into the sand and shoved the bits deeply.

As they worked, they discussed their predicament in low

59

whispers. Ed Coulton said: "When do we make our break?"

"I dunno. These ain't fools . . . even if they are lazy. They knew, when they put these spades in our hands, that we'd start thinking what we could do with them . . . and they'll just be waitin' for us to try." Bill rammed the tool deeply into the sand with his boot, tossed aside a spadeful of the loose and gritty stuff. They had sunk their well a couple of feet now and there was still no dark sign of moisture. Perhaps a table of impervious rock underlay this creekbed.

A hot wind eddied through, swirling the loose sand into their faces. Coulton cursed and spat it from his mouth.

Duke called across from the shadows: "Keep workin'!"

"The hell with you!" Ed Coulton straightened, running the back of a hand across his sweaty jowls. "It's hot, here in the sun. How about a swig from one of them canteens?"

The gunman pointed at the hole. "Dig it, and you can drink it! We got no more than we need for ourselves!"

Ed glowered at him, and began stripping out of his sweat-soaked shirt. Bill was already bare to the waist, his torso feeling the strong weight of the sun as he bent and lifted to the unfamiliar labor of digging.

"The crooks are probably in Enid right now," Ed Coulton muttered. "Recording our claims."

His friend said nothing. Emery's brain had been hunting futilely for any out. But he could think of nothing that had any chance of succeeding against the wary caution of the gunmen. And the same bitter impatience that he could read in Coulton's manner was having its way with him. Time was running away from them; shadows were already starting to lengthen in the bottom of the dry bed.

Now, at last, the searching spade bits found sand that was more compact, more resistant, and dark with moisture. They went to the work with renewed energy, and in a moment a small seepage of muddy-looking water began to fill the bottom of the hole as they withdrew the tools. Bill Emery laid his spade aside and went to his knees, scooped the hole out with his hand. He brought his fingers up at last, cupped and dripping, and tasted the warm, brackish liquid.

"Well, there you are!" he called to the guards as he wiped his hands upon his jeans. "It's wet, anyhow. Can't say much more than that for it!"

Griffen and Duke got unhurriedly to their feet and came over to see the well. Ed Coulton was mopping his face on his discarded shirt; Emery, still on his knees, waited with one hand resting on the spade handle beside him, the other in the loose sand.

As Duke stopped, leaning forward slightly to look into the hole that was slowly filling with water, Emery suddenly lunged upward, grabbing up the spade while his free hand flung dry gritty sand directly into the gunman's face.

V

But luck was not with him. A vagrant breath of wind, playing along the creekbed, chose that moment to lift a gust that tore the sand from Emery's fingers, and whipped it away before it touched its target. With a dull despair, knowing he had missed the chance of temporarily blinding his enemy, he brought the spade up in an arc, hoping to catch Duke on the side of the head or perhaps knock the gun from his hand. As he did so, his body braced itself for the expected shock of a bullet.

His wild swing with the spade missed completely, for Duke had dodged backward when the handful of grit leaped toward him. With Emery flung off balance, Duke held his fire and instead brought the gun's barrel down, hard. It struck the other's arm, numbing it to the shoulder, letting the spade fall uselessly to the ground. "Tricky!" snarled the Duke. "You need teachin', I reckon!"

He waded forward and a heavy fist connected with Emery's jaw, drove him half around. Bill caught himself, boots sliding in the loose soil, and swung both fists. His left, still numb from the clubbing of the six-gun, felt nothing when it struck Duke's body with little steam behind it, but the other took his enemy on the side of the head and visibly jarred him. Breath gusted from his parted lips.

Then, with an angry grunt, Duke brought the gun barrel down again. It landed at the point where Emery's neck joined his body, and agony exploded all through him. He dropped, unable to hold himself up. In the half dark of slipping consciousness, he lay and felt the slam of a boot.

"I oughta plug you!" he heard Duke's harsh voice saying. "I would, if Morgan hadn't said otherwise."

There was mumbled talk between the two gunmen that Bill Emery was too far gone to understand. Finally a hand fastened itself in his hair, and he was dragged that way to the edge of the well and his head dropped into it, into the brackish water rising within the hole. The shock of it revived him somewhat, set him struggling feebly to lift his face out of the water.

"Give your pal a hand," Griffen's voice ordered. "Get him on his feet."

It was Ed Coulton that hauled him to a sitting position. When Bill blinked the water out of his eyes and things stopped their dizzy spinning, he saw Ed's face beside him and Ed's mouth was working, tears of rage running down his cheeks. "Damn them!" he cried. "I never had a chance to help you, Bill. That Griffen, and his rifle. . . ."

"Up!" snapped Duke. "Hurry it!"

Although his body was still gripped with weakness, Bill managed with Ed's help to get his feet under him. Ed picked up his friend's shirt and handed it to him, then, on orders, collected the spades and slung them on his own shoulder.

"All right," said Duke. "Start back. And no more monkey business out of either of you, or I'll forget what Morgan told me. Understand?"

The first few steps, Bill Emery thought he wouldn't be able to make it. But after Ed had helped him up the creekbank, he found his strength returning. His neck ached so he could scarcely turn his head; he only slowly reassured himself that the clubbing, and the boot against his side, hadn't done some severe internal damage. With the gunmen prodding him, he managed to keep walking, stumbling and uncertain, and gradually he got surer control of himself.

They reached the main house, marched past it toward the bunkshack dug-out. Barely had they cleared the corner of the building when someone called sharply: "Drop them weepons and turn around, damn you!"

It was Mac McIvor's voice! It halted all four in their tracks, and a curse came from one of Banning's men. Then the gunmen were spinning about, and past them Bill Emery caught a glimpse of the old cowpuncher, standing with his back against the ranch house wall, the bandage around his head and a six-gun in his fingers. There wasn't time to wonder where he had managed to get hold of a gun. He saw that Banning's men intended shooting it out; he heard a cry on his own lips that was lost in the quick mingling of gunfire.

Duke's revolver roared a fraction of a second ahead of McIvor's, but his shot was wild, and he had no time for a second one. He doubled over to the pound of lead into him, and fell, knocked backward against Emery's legs. Bill saw the gun he had dropped, spinning in the dirt; he went after it, landing on all fours and grabbing up the weapon.

At the same instant he heard a *clang* of metal. Ed Coulton, swinging both the spades he carried over his shoulder, had brought them chopping down across the barrel of Griffen's rifle just as the man was about to make a hip shot at the old man by the house. The Winchester spilled from his hands, but Griffen wore a holstered six-shooter and he cursed as he pulled for it, backing away from the reach of Coulton's swinging spades.

He had it out of the holster, was bringing it into line on Ed Coulton when Bill Emery got Duke's six-gun into his hand and, with an elbow against the ground, triggered twice. He aimed for Griffen's arm and the first bullet missed; the second, taking him dead center, hurled Griffen around and dropped him on his face, dead before he hit the ground.

The quick racket of the shots died in echoes along the hill above the ranch. Slowly, shakily Bill got to his knees, and then his feet. Ed looked stunned by the rapid turn of events. Over at the house, old Mac was slowly sagging, sliding down the rough logs of the wall.

His own weakness forgotten, Bill got to him and threw an arm around him. He thought Duke's bullet might have tallied, but he saw no blood. Then Mac opened his eyes and blinked a little, and shook his head. "By gonnies," he muttered. "That gun had a bigger kick than I was ready for. It jarred me, and I hit the back of my head against a log. Thought I was gonna pass out. . . ."

Bill looked down at the revolver Mac had let drop to his feet. He stooped and picked it up, astonished. "Why, this is my six-gun. Where'd you get it, Mac?"

"Found it in the bunk, right beside me. I come to a bit ago, and I was layin' practically on it."

"In the bunk?" Emery put a puzzled look on Ed Coulton, who had joined them, carrying Griffen's rifle and revolver. "But, I don't get this? I. . . ." His eyes widened as it hit him. "The girl! *She* took it off me, when she turned us over to Banning. She must have hung onto it, and sneaked it into the dug-out when she went in there to patch up Mac's hurt."

Coulton shook his head, incredulous. "That don't sound likely."

"But it must be! It's the only explanation! My God, do you suppose . . . ?" A lift of feeling made him grip Ed Coulton's arm. "She only turned us in because she was afraid we'd try to hold out, and Banning would murder us. Later, by sneaking this gun where she was sure we'd find it, she figured we could use it to escape. It *must* be that, Ed. We figured wrong about her. Laura's on our side, after all."

Ed Coulton's manner didn't thaw. "You're forgettin' a few things. For one, it was her that sold us down the river by telling Banning our plans. For another, her name ain't Laura

Cain . . . it's Belle Conway, and she's Banning's girl. You can't get around that."

The surge of warmth in Bill Emery died slowly. For just an instant he felt that he almost hated Ed for reminding him of these facts, yet there they were. And yet, again, it did look as though Laura—he somehow couldn't stop thinking of her by that name—had deliberately crossed Morgan Banning in order to aid them. Otherwise, where had that gun come from?

It was a riddle. He shook his head, deciding it was too tough for him to answer, then a squint at the hang of the sun brought him back to their immediate problem. "We've got no time to stand around here arguing," he said. "It's a long ride to Enid . . . and that's where we ought to be, right now! Let's tote these bodies into the dug-out and then get started."

Only one of the Sooner's broncos still remained in the corral. Their own horses had stayed in the vicinity of the ranch, however, and had been grazing and seemed rested enough after the run. A drink from the well, filling nicely as ground water seeped into it, and they seemed ready to take the trail.

McIvor insisted that he was in shape to ride. "I got nothin' to wait around here for," he pointed out. "My old head feels all right now, and, if I don't go along, I'll do nothin' but worry." So they didn't argue with him.

Bill Emery's own body was stiff and sore, and he didn't like to move his shoulder any more than was necessary. He had to grit his teeth a little as he tightened the cinches on the piebald gelding, and lifted himself into the saddle. After that, the three of them were ready to ride.

They passed through a land that had altered strangely in half a day. Where this morning there had been only empty grass, inhabited by deer and coyotes and the other wild things of the prairie, now every quarter section of the Cherokee

Strip had its occupant. Here, a man was toiling at the digging of a well; yonder, a family of land seekers had taken the canvas cover from their furniture-laden wagon and were setting it up to make a tent. The sound of an axe rang from a grove of cottonwood where someone was knocking up firewood, or timber for the beginning of a house.

There were other sounds—the angry shouts of men contesting a disputed claim, and once or twice a crackling of gunfire that drifted across the prairie startlingly. As they trailed down into a wooded hollow, they found the body of a man hanging from a stout tree limb, the shadow of drought-crisped leaves flickering over him as he twisted slowly on the end of a creaking rope. His face, with the horror of strangulation in its popping eyes and gaping mouth, was not pretty to look upon.

A piece of paper had been pinned to his shirt front and the crudely penciled words told their story simply enough: **Too damn soon!**

It was already coming dark when they rode into the new town of Enid, and here were even wilder sights than they had witnessed elsewhere. The entire town site had been claimed, regardless of the fact that some of the lots staked would have to be forfeited to make way for streets. In a sea of torchlight and noise, men swarmed over the place. Its only wooden structures were the railroad depot and a Land Office, but already the heavy freight wagons were rolling across the Strip, hauling in lumber and supplies, and the sound of saw and hammer mingled with the raucous voice of the new town, as the framework of rough wooden buildings began to go up. For the rest, Enid was a place of hurriedly pitched tents and of campfires on the open prairie.

They threaded their way through this confusion, hunting the Land Office, and found it by the long tail of land seekers that was queued up in front of it. "Hold up here," Bill Emery muttered and, swinging down, passed his reins to Ed Coulton. Hand on gun butt, he approached the line of people waiting to file their claims. His glance searched for a face he recognized, ready for trouble the instant he ran across it. He hardly expected to find Banning or any of his men, however, and in this he was right. After a quick but careful survey, he returned to his friends, shaking his head.

"No sign of them here," he reported, again rising to the saddle. "They've had time enough to record the claims, long since."

Ed shifted tiredly in the leather, his long face scowling. "They've headed back to Figure Eight already, then. We passed them somewhere."

"Maybe. But I don't think so. I have an idea they're still in town."

"How can we expect to find them, if they are?" Ed Coulton flung a hand, indicating all the jam-packed mass of men and horses boiling through the raw tent city.

"I dunno yet, for sure."

Actually Bill was not as convinced as he had sounded that Banning hadn't left Enid. But a look at old Mac had convinced him that the oldster hadn't the strength in him to ride any farther tonight. McIvor was saying nothing, but the way he sagged over the neck of his bronco, one veined hand clamped to the saddle pommel, was enough to show that his head wound had begun telling on him again.

To spare the old man's feelings, therefore, Bill Emery said: "I'm gonna look around, anyway. These bronc's of ours have taken a beating today and they need a rest, and some grain if we can find any. Mac, I suggest you stick around and keep a sharp eye on them, or some smart cookie might take a notion to them and try to set us afoot."

It was almost pathetic, the way McIvor agreed with this suggestion. He was really near the tag end of his strength, and his head probably felt as though it had split open like a melon. Bill himself was feeling cranky and sore in every muscle. That bullet scratch on his leg was beginning to pain him again. He was glad that Ed didn't seem inclined to argue.

They cast about, and finally located a place where they could strike saddles and make a camp of sorts. Bill had some cold grub in his saddlebags and they shared this, together with what was left of their water.

As the night deepened, the tumult and din of this raw place seemed to grow even stronger. Bill Emery, remembering nights that were gone forever—fine, free nights when the Cherokee Strip had been the last open range and a man could ride the starlit prairies in utter stillness and the company of his own large thoughts—felt a kind of sickness at what he found about him now.

Of course, this would pass; the thugs and speculators who swarmed to such a place as this would soon scatter, and a real town would grow on this wild spot and settle into a future of prosperity and peace. But the past that Bill Emery remembered had had its own beauty, and it would fade but slowly before the inexorable march of what men called civilization.

His meager meal finished, he hitched up his jeans and asked Ed Coulton: "Ready to start huntin'? I got an idea or two . . . from something Banning said this afternoon. Let's head over to the railroad depot."

Here, there was another jostling swarm of men; a train that had just pulled in was disgorging a new load of the land hungry, and carloads of every sort of supplies. Emery and Coulton pushed their way through the crowd around the big engine that exuded steam and the odor of heated metal, and sought the telegrapher's window.

A tired-looking man, in a sweated-out shirt, looked up irritably from the key and the stack of penciled sheets in front of him. He shook his head at Emery's question.

"Don't ask me about any wire I sent out today!" he groaned. "I've worked this key until my wrist will be in a sling for a month. And no end to it!" He picked up a message just completed, from the top of the pile, and speared it on a nail that already held a mass of the yellow sheets.

"Are all of them on this hook?"

"Yeah . . . but I got no authority to let you go pawing through that stack."

"Take it easy," said Bill. "I ain't hurting you any."

The man was too busy and too tired and too pressed with work to take time arguing about it. Bill started thumbing back through the smudged and scribbled sheets; he hardly expected to find anything, but he did know Morgan Banning had spoken of wiring an order for supplies from Dodge. And sure enough, suddenly he was staring at a message scrawled in a strong, powerful hand above Banning's signature.

The order was for food, lumber, nails, and such; also, he requested a surveying crew to be sent down as soon as possible. Obviously Banning meant to waste no time getting started on the layout of his town. What interested Bill Emery were the last few words of the telegram: **Wire reply collect here at the Golden Parrot.**

"What's this Golden Parrot?" he asked the operator. "Sounds like a saloon."

The other shrugged. "There's at least twenty or thirty of them started up since noon . . . I can't lay off long enough for a beer!"

Emery turned to his friend. "Come on! That's one way to make your head save your heels," he observed. "We got Banning treed now. All we have to do is locate this saloon where he's waiting for word from Dodge."

"Maybe he's already had his answer."

"I'll bet not, with the wires as jammed as they are. Let's go looking for him."

It was a matter of hunting blindly through that sprawling confusion of campfires, of tents with the cherry glow of lantern light staining their canvas sides, of men and animals and wagons shuttling through the dry, fire-reddened dust. Several men they asked could give no more answer than a shrug of shoulders; there were too many whiskey mills sprung up, like poisonous mushrooms, for a single one to be easily found or remembered.

But then a tip steered them in the right direction, and at last they found it—a huge tent of dirty brown canvas with sides rolled up to let some air circulate through its interior and with a painted sign raised across the front entrance with a crude yellow painting of a bird. Brawling racket that poured out of this place struck them almost with a physical force; it was like wading into a strong current, as they shouldered their way through the flow of traffic into the tent.

It had no floor; the odor of dust and of sun-dried grass trampled under many boots rose to mingle with smells of sweat and of sour, cheap booze. Gasoline lanterns hung in clusters from every upright post to give light. Along both sides of the tent, planks set on sawhorses formed long makeshift bars, where a battery of aproned bartenders ladled whiskey from open barrels.

Looking over the men that crowded the place, Bill Emery thought—as he had often enough before in his inspection of this newborn town—that the scourings of a dozen cities' tough sections must have poured in here. He saw depraved and evil faces under the hard hats of city crooks and sharpers; they had flocked like buzzards to the pickings, and they

71

would have to be cleaned out before Enid, and the other new towns of the Strip, could settle to the business of growth and establishment. For the time being, they were in the majority—outnumbering the honest ones who had come here with the serious purpose of building for the years to come.

And then, Ed Coulton's fingers were tightening on his shoulder and he heard Ed's hoarse exclamation: "Watch it! There's Banning . . . yonder. And that woman is with him!"

VI

Toward the rear of the tent, tables and chairs had been set out and card games were in progress there—islands of relative quiet, amid the din and stir of the crowded tent. It was at one of these tables that Ed Coulton had spied their quarry, seated facing them. Morgan Banning, with Stetson pushed back from his florid, handsome face and a cigar clamped between his teeth, was studying a five-card poker hand as he juggled a stack of chips, debating his play.

Four other men of a similar stripe were seated about the table; a sizeable pot had already been built in the center of it. Ed, looking at them closely, muttered: "That ain't none of the crew Banning had with him at Figure Eight, and I don't spot any of them in the crowd. But they're bound to be handy."

Bill scarcely heard him. His whole attention was on the sixth person seated at the poker table. Laura Cain was not playing. She merely sat there at Banning's elbow, her hands in her lap, looking small and lost, the only woman in all that crowd of drunken, raucous humanity.

He tried to remind himself cynically that this was, after all, a natural milieu with her—that she was Banning's girl, the Belle Conway who entertained in the Dodge City saloon, but somehow he couldn't reconcile this thought with the sight of her sitting there. Perhaps it was only wishful imagination that found unhappiness in her pale features—even fear.

Almost without thinking, he slipped his gun from its holster. Ed had the six-gun they had taken off the dead outlaw, Duke. He palmed this in his hard, bony hand. Bill Emery said: "All right. Let's take him."

73

It was the girl who saw them first, moving through the crowd, shoving men aside as they bore directly in upon the table. Bill saw her stiffen, saw her bosom lift to a quickly drawn breath. Sight of them must have been startling enough to jar a gasp from her, because Morgan Banning turned and looked at her and then, seeing where her staring eyes were fixed, swung his own glance in that direction.

Thus he met the savage fury in the two who approached, guns ready, and for just a fraction of a second he remained frozen that way, stunned by the unexpectedness of it. For an instant only. Morgan Banning was a man of quick reactions, and now his astonishment gave way to a look of rage. But he must have decided that the odds were too heavily against him from a pair of guns already drawn and leveled.

He did not hesitate, or make a futile try for a weapon of his own. Instead, with savage anger he flung his cards from him and his knee came up; a boot was placed against the edge of the table and with a hard thrust he drove it from him, toppling it fully upon the players seated opposite. There was a cascading of chips and cards and whiskey glasses; a man was carried backwards to the ground as his chair went over with him.

Bill Emery cursed as he saw the strategy. For instantly, as those nearest the table were driven back, they surged against him and Ed Coulton, clotted into a wall of sweaty bodies that, for the moment, they could not penetrate however they fought to tear through.

Meanwhile, Banning was on his feet. Between the heads of the men who held him back, Bill saw the saloon man kick aside his chair. He had palmed a gun now; with the other hand he seized Laura Cain's wrist and hauled her after him, as he started for the rear exit and the dark night beyond.

"Let me through! Damn you!" Bill heard his own panting

voice, as he pawed and tore at the press of men. Someone turned and cursed him, and a fist struck his cheek and raised the blood.

But then he was free with a suddenness that made his boots slip on the slick, trodden grass and hurl him to one knee. He scrambled instantly to his feet, and went running toward that dark opening in the rear wall of the tent where Banning and the girl had vanished.

He had to haul up here a moment, made uncertain after the blaze of lights inside the tent. Someone joined him, and Ed Coulton was panting, close at his elbow: "Where'd they go? We lose 'em again?"

"There," Emery grunted suddenly.

His eyes, accustoming themselves to the star glow and the spotted reflections of scattered campfires, had picked out a pair of figures in the shadows, some 100 feet away. They appeared to be struggling; he heard a man's hard breathing, a woman's sob. The girl was fighting Morgan Banning, hauling back and trying to break loose of the grip on her arm.

Banning, held back by her, was likely growing desperate. Suddenly the two listening heard the sharp, clear impact of an open-handed slap. Laura Cain ceased her struggling, and next moment they had melted into the night.

Held breath had gusted out of Bill Emery, hearing that stinging slap. Beside him came Ed's exclamation: "Why, the dirty son-of-a-bitch!" Bill found his own hand clamped tightly about his six-gun butt; he could not have fired, though, without endangering the girl. "Come on," he gritted, and they both lunged forward in the wake of the vanished pair.

They had gone only a half dozen paces when gunfire opened up unexpectedly behind them.

Whirling, they dived for the ground to escape the wild

screaming of bullets overhead. Behind them, near the saloon tent, red fire lanced from the guns of a couple of silhouetted figures. Even in that poor light, Emery was sure they were two of Morgan Banning's claim jumpers who had stolen Figure 8. Probably they had been inside the Golden Parrot and he had missed spotting them in the crowd.

On one knee, crouched low to the dark ground, he started working his own six-shooter, and an instant later Ed Coulton's weapon joined his. Men who had started out of the saloon tent yelled and pulled back inside again. A lamp hanging from a post took a wild bullet and was smashed, dangling there and dripping burning oil.

It was furious shooting but inaccurate in the dark. Then Emery caught one of that pair between his gun and the tent's lighted canvas, and he punched out a bullet that took the man squarely. He spun and collapsed, and his companion took warning and went for better cover.

Ed Coulton gritted: "I'll take care of the other one. You get after Banning."

Bill needed no urging. "Right," he said, and, coming to his feet, started running in the direction he thought his enemy had taken. Behind him, as he went, he heard Ed's gun starting again.

There was no sign of Banning, or the girl. He hauled up a moment, considering, while his busy hands kicked empty shells from the reeking six-gun, fed in new ones from his loop belt. Chagrin filled him. It began to look very much as though that moment's delay had been fatal, that he had lost them for sure—and Banning wouldn't be so easy to find a second time. He would keep out of sight and wait for a chance to back shoot his enemy while Bill, in turn, was hunting for him. Emery clicked the loading gate shut, palmed the gun in a steady hand.

He prowled forward, then, casting blindly. Hampered by his prisoner, Banning couldn't have made too much time. He skirted a wagon, moved between a pair of tents and past a cook fire, drew back quickly as a drunken horsebacker larruped past him, whooping and reeling in the saddle and narrowly missing a collision. No sign of Banning anywhere, or of the girl. A cold sweat formed on him and he broke into a sprint.

Then, from somewhere at his right, he heard a sound, the sobbing of a woman. It pulled him sharply about. Here there was another fire, and a clot of horses near it, and the figures of men. Two men, one standing motionlessly, holding rein leathers; the other was Morgan Banning, and, as Bill Emery saw him, he was trying to force the girl to mount a saddle. Emery's jaw set hard.

"Banning!" he shouted. "Let go of her, and turn around!"

For an instant only Banning froze, the impact of the order hitting him. Hard red soil crunched under Emery's boots as he ran forward, gun leveled, but not daring to shoot with the girl there. Then Laura Cain had managed to jerk free of Banning who, before Emery could get off a shot, turned and, moving quickly, placed one of the saddled horses between him and his approaching enemy.

Firelight gleamed on his angry, handsome face, glittered on the gun barrel he dropped across the saddle for a quick shot.

At first, Emery thought his gun hand had been smashed with a sudden, clubbing blow. He halted in his tracks, almost spun around by the force of it, looked dully at his numbed and aching fingers, taking a moment to realize that they were empty and that Banning's slug had chanced to strike the gun and knock it spinning.

He looked for the six-shooter on the ground, and failed to

find it. Then, lifting his head, he saw Banning's face again—twisted in triumph now—and the gun leveling for a second, finishing shot. Still dazed a little, he could recognize death when he saw it looking at him, when he knew he had no chance of beating it out, no choice but to stand and wait.

"No, Banning!"

That other man—the one, Bill remembered suddenly, that had looked strangely familiar even in a glimpse of him riding away from Figure 8 to stake the stolen claims—was lunging at his boss, reaching for Banning's gun arm. In amazement, Bill Emery recognized him this time, even as he saw that Johnny Haig had no gun and that Banning was turning on him in fury.

"Keep back, you damned fool!" cried Banning, backing a step before Johnny Haig's reckless advance, his revolver swinging on him. "I warned you. . . ."

"I've let you turn me into a traitor," shouted Johnny Haig, "but I won't stand by and . . . !"

The six-shooter in Banning's hand leaped, spouting red flame. Johnny took the shot head-on, at a distance of little more than a yard. It stopped him in his tracks, drove him back a pace. Then his hands came up, clawing at his middle; slowly he doubled forward, and crashed face downward to the ground.

Laura Cain's scream mingled with the echoes of the shot. The horses, terrified by the noise of the gun, shied wildly and scattered; they left Morgan Banning for the moment exposed.

Bill Emery, hurling himself full length, swept up his gun which he had finally sighted, where Banning's slug had flung it from his hand. He felt the muscles of his face, hard and stiff as a mask, pulling his lips back from set teeth in a grimace as he propped his elbows against the earth and laid the muzzle of his gun against Morgan Banning's hated, fire-lit shape. He worked the trigger twice, three times, without stopping to debate whether every bullet he fired was needed.

Then he held his hand and acrid smoke filmed away, and there was nothing before his gun. Slowly he lowered it, and came up to his knees, and then climbed to his feet. After the racket of the shots, the noise of this raw, newborn town seemed dim and faraway. It had swallowed up this moment of violence and seemed to care not at all, or even to have noticed.

He walked over for a glance at Banning, a glance being all he needed to know the man was dead. He turned then and knelt beside Johnny Haig, and gently eased him over to his back. He tried not to look at what Banning's lead had done to him, but rather at the sweaty, pain-tightened features of this man who had once been his friend.

Johnny felt the touch, and his eyes wavered open. "That you . . . Bill?" he whispered with effort. "You all right?"

"Sure. Sure, Johnny." He swallowed. "Does it hurt?"

The other's head waggled a little from side to side. "Don't seem to . . . feel a thing. Listen, Bill. I'm sorry for . . . what I done. I missed connections with Ed, there in Dodge City, and wound up at Banning's place, and started playing poker. Lost more'n I could pay off. And that ain't a healthy thing to do, when it's Morgan Banning you're dealing with."

"I understand, Johnny. I figured it was about like that. Don't talk about it."

But Johnny, with dying strength, was determined on a full confession. "I heard myself blabbing everything about our plans for the old Figure Eight . . . selling the rest of you downriver to save my own neck. The more he heard, the more he sounded interested. But he said I'd have to ride with him and the others. To show the way . . . get across at night, and be on the ground before the run started." The words tumbled out of him. "Today, when you showed up, there was a gun on me to stop me trying to yell a warning. After the shooting was over, Banning told me old Mac wasn't too bad hurt, and the three of you would all be set free as soon as the claims were registered. And he promised again, if I kept on doing what I was told and making myself useful, I'd be well taken care of. Bill, I still wanted to believe him. And tonight, when I saw you and Ed walk into that tent, I thought it meant Morgan Banning had kept his word . . . until the shooting started and I knew I'd been a fool, all along. And . . . and I was so ashamed."

"No need for that," Emery said gruffly. "Whatever you did wrong, you've more than made up for it." But he could see only too well that Johnny was slipping away from him. He made a last effort to get through. "Listen . . . can you tell me if Banning and his men, after jumping our claims, got around to registering them?"

He thought at first his words hadn't reached Johnny, but then the answer came, slow and muffled: "Naw . . . he said they'd wait till it cooled off some and the lines got shorter. No reason they should stand for hours in the sun . . . like all those damn' fools who actually made the run today. . . ." After that, there was nothing more. Bill Emery felt his lungs swell, reaching for air as sudden, choking grief constricted them.

A thousand memories poured in upon him, engulfing him. Johnny had been weak—as weak as water. But he'd ridden range with Bill and Ed and Mac, and shared their grub and saddle blankets—and those things you didn't forget. Besides, Johnny had indeed paid off his score, at the last minute—and paid it with his own life.

Then Bill Emery felt the girl's hand upon his shoulder. "You can't do anything for him now, Bill."

"No." He rose, facing her. "Laura," he began, then corrected himself "or Belle . . . or whatever your name is. . . ."

"It's Laura Cain, Bill . . . just as I told you yesterday evening. Everything I said then was the truth . . . about my mother, and my sisters. Only there were some things I didn't tell . . . because I was hoping I could forget them."

"Then forget them now," he said quickly. "I'm not asking questions, Laura."

"But I want you to know it all. About . . . him." She indicated, without looking, the still form of Morgan Banning on the ground behind her. "You heard me called by the name of Belle Conway . . . the name I used when I went into Dodge and found a job at Banning's place, singing to earn money my family needed so desperately. You've heard me spoken of as Morgan Banning's woman, but that part isn't true . . . not . . . not the way they mean it. I. . . ." She looked away, and there was shame and the need of confession in the words as she forced them out, in a small and dismal voice. "I did let him make love to me. I couldn't help it. There was something about his voice, and his hands . . . something I wasn't able to. . . . But you must believe me, Bill, that I . . . that we were never. . . ."

"I believe you, Laura," he told her quickly.

"Finally I knew I had to get free of him. So I ran away from him, and came to try my chances in the Cherokee Strip. I was desperate, and it was the only thing I knew to save myself. And he . . . followed me. I don't know how he learned where I was. Through the man who drove my wagon down to the starting line, most likely. Anyway, he found me last night and begged me to come back. And for a moment he . . . almost won." She added: "I didn't know about Johnny Haig, about Morgan's plan to take Figure Eight for himself . . . not until I heard his voice shouting from the ranch house. I knew what

81

you thought when I took your gun and made you surrender
. . . but I was only trying to save your lives."

Bill Emery touched her arm. Before he could answer her,
they were interrupted by someone who came running toward
them through the darkness. It was Ed Coulton, still carrying
the smoking gun with which he had killed the last of Morgan
Banning's Sooners. He shouted Bill's name, came to a
sudden stop staring at the bodies.

Ed leaned for a close look at Johnny Haig's still face,
straightened up with a stunned look, searching Bill's eyes for
confirmation. "Was . . . was it him . . . ?"

At Emery's solemn nod, a kind of sickness passed over Ed
Coulton's bony features. Then he looked at Laura and his expression changed, became contrite. "I guess, then, that I
wronged you, ma'am. I'm sorry."

"Please don't apologize," she said. "You could hardly
have thought anything else." Suddenly she was weeping, and
Bill Emery found his arms about her, her head against his
chest, his own body feeling the sobs that shook hers. "You see
now why I hate towns! The things I've seen here, and at
Dodge. . . ."

"It won't be like that in our town," he promised her with
conviction. "We'll keep the Morgan Bannings out. We'll
make it a place where honest men can bring their families,
and do their trading, and have a decent life."

She lifted her head, looking at him with a small, puzzled
frown. "I thought you weren't staying? I thought you were
going to make a stake and push on West where there's room
and nobody crowding you?"

Bill Emery grinned a little. "Maybe I don't feel that way
now. Maybe I want to stick around . . . be a part of all the
changes that are coming to the old Cherokee Strip. Or
maybe. . . ." He hesitated, suddenly afraid to hear her answer.

"If I thought that you would be here, and that it made any difference to you whether I went or stayed. . . ."

She spoke his name breathlessly. And suddenly he forgot this wild town of Enid that lay about them—forgot everything except the girl he held in his arms.

As he bent to kiss her, he murmured: "Honey, I wonder if there was any preachers made the run this morning . . . and how quick can we find one?"

Range of No Return

1

The salt cedars that dropped above the post office at Denison had found, somewhere, enough breeze to stir their feathery branches. In the hot, choking blast of afternoon, they made a small whisper of sound as they dragged against the walls of the building, across the tin of the arcade roof that fronted it.

Standing on the step in the shade of the roof, big Walt Hubbard heard the whisper, gauged the strength of the breeze that caused it, and thought not too hopefully of rain. The stocky, middle-aged rancher had a soggy handkerchief in one hand, with which at intervals he mopped the sweat from a red-burned neck, tilting up his head and reaching inside the open shirt collar to do so. It was July, and hotter than hell. Hubbard's foreman, Charlie Moss, came out of the post office and joined his boss, one hand full of letters. There was a smoldering glint in his eyes that flared higher as he squinted across the rutted street, at the big rambling barn that passed for a county courthouse.

"Has he come out yet?" the foreman demanded tautly.

The Bar H owner frowned, following the other's glance to the glass-paneled side door marked Sheriff's Office. Both of them looked at the dusty coat of the black horse, waiting hip-shot at the hitching pole in front of it.

Hubbard shook his head. "No," he said a little reluctantly. "He's still in there."

The foreman cursed. His voice sounded flat and small against the immense heat of the day, but the anger that pulsed through his body made the corded muscles of his arms stand out as he clenched his fists tightly. "We ought to go drag him out . . . him and that turncoat sheriff."

"Quit it," Walt Hubbard snapped. "Nobody drawin' Bar H pay is gonna take sides in a thing that don't concern 'em. I mean that, Charlie."

With an effort Charlie Moss calmed. The letters in his taut hand were badly crushed. He scowled at them, stuffed them into a pocket of his leather vest that was worked with porcupine quills. "The idea of that Cole *hombre* comin' back to take up on this range," he muttered through his teeth. "If that don't concern Bar H, I dunno what would. Was old Tom Ward still alive, he'd see to it that. . . ."

"I said quit it!" The Bar H boss' voice was really sharp this time. Usually soft spoken, when he sounded like that you knew that he meant it, and the foreman wisely put a clamp on his tongue. Lantern jaw shot forward, Moss fell silent.

Hubbard dabbed at his neck again with the handkerchief and put his glance out to the horizon, beyond the adobes and dirty frame houses of the town. Over vermilion cliffs, far distant, a few unimportant puffs of cloud hung in the dead stillness of the upper air. The rest of the sky in that part of Arizona was blank, clear, and of a brightness that hurt the eyes.

Along the road that snaked away across the tawny yellow of the range, a dust cloud was rolling that most obviously was not a product of any breeze. Hubbard had been eyeing its approach for several minutes, off and on, watching it grow. He could see the light buckboard and team that centered it, and the small figure alone on the seat.

If that's who I think it is, he thought, *we may be in for some fireworks.*

Still scowling, Charlie Moss paired his glance with his own perpetual squint. The dust cloud had almost reached the rim of town by now, and through the drifting brown curtains they made out a splash of green that was the dress of the girl who drove it. "It's Betty Ward!" he exclaimed suddenly. "Reckon she's heard . . . ?"

Hubbard said: "Don't see how she could have, so soon, although there's been rumors it was gonna happen. I dunno. She's in a powerful hurry." He looked sharply at his foreman. "But, remember, we're stayin' out of this."

Charlie Moss said nothing, but he spat into the pool of dust at his feet.

In a few moments, the buckboard had tooled to a halt directly in front of the post office where they stood. Both men nodded and touched hat brims. The girl on the seat nodded in turn, pushed back her sombrero to let some of the thick black curls tumble across her forehead. She looked surprisingly cool, refreshing. But there wasn't any misjudging, either, the hot glint of anger that struck sparks in her brown eyes.

"Hello, Walt," she said briefly. "Charlie." She turned her head, glanced across at the dreary bulk of the courthouse, then back again. "The sheriff in?" she asked.

The men exchanged looks. Charlie Moss moistened his lips with his tongue. It was Hubbard who answered. "Reckon he is, Betty." He added: "But I think he's got company. . . ."

Betty Ward didn't seem to hear that last. She was already leaping down from the seat of the buckboard. She gave Hubbard a—"Thanks."—over her shoulder, and started across the hot stretch of the road.

Moss made a move forward. He stopped as the hand of his boss tightened on his wrist. He scowled, but did not speak.

The girl went on without looking back. Her small body seemed filled with one purpose, her pretty, dark head set on one idea. She skirted around the big black hitched at the sheriff's rack, without seeming to notice it, stepped up on the rough plank sidewalk, put a hand on the rusted doorknob, and pushed inside the office.

It was a tiny cubbyhole occupying one corner of the courthouse building, and it was very dark after the full blast of the street glare. But Betty Ward could see the lawman seated at his desk under the window and she went straight to him.

Lew Duncan's jaw sagged a bit in consternation at her entrance. He sat forward quickly, putting down the papers he had in his hand and jerking rimless glasses from his eyes. Under bushy brows his shrewd glance stabbed at her. "Uh . . . 'afternoon," he said.

She didn't wait for formalities. She brushed the word away with one small, brown hand and said levelly, her eyes snapping: "I've heard! I've heard what they're saying. And if you do it . . . if you've got the gall. . . ."

The sheriff ran a fleshy hand across his bald spot. "Whoa, Betty. Rein up. Lemme know what you're talkin' about."

"You know, all right," she flashed back at him. "That thief! That . . . that varmint, Herb Cole. They say you've the nerve to invite him back here to Denison. Just as though nothing had ever happened. Is that true?"

Very carefully the sheriff set his glasses down on the scarred desk top. "Suppose it is?" he said, choosing his words deliberately. "Suppose I have told him to come home? Where's the harm of it? The case against him has been dropped. There's no evidence."

"There was, five years ago," Betty Ward reminded him. "There was plenty of evidence. Even an eyewitness who saw the crook in the act of changing my uncle's brand. If Herb Cole hadn't sneaked across the border when he did, he'd be in prison this minute . . . where he belongs."

"The witness is dead," Lew Duncan pointed out quietly. "Your uncle is dead. The whole case is a past issue."

"And, meanwhile, Herb Cole has a ranch in this county

that's been waiting five years for him." The girl's anger tied her tongue for a moment. "Well," she managed finally, "if that's how it is . . . if the law's backing rustlers now. . . . But let me tell you one thing, Lew Duncan. Don't think, just because a girl owns Flying W, that it isn't still a fighting spread. My uncle never liked rustlers for neighbors. Neither do I. And I want to know what Herb Cole expects to do after he comes back. Take up right where he left off? Break out his running iron again?"

"Why, as for that," said a voice behind her calmly, "I reckon I'm in a better position than the sheriff is, ma'am, for tellin' you what I'm aiming to do."

The girl spun quickly, stared at the man who stood at the office's inner door. He was a tall man, and rather lean. The gray eyes that looked at her had a quality something like a slow acid, eating into any face they rested on, but gradually, so quietly that the burn of them wasn't noticed at first. There might have been a touch of humor about his mouth, once, but something had pinched it out.

The hand, laid on the knob of the door he had just opened, was big, heavy, rope-scarred. "I'm afraid I got home a little earlier than I was expected, Miss Ward," Herb Cole said.

Betty's anger seemed to flare as the acid of his glance rested on her. She whirled on the sheriff. "You knew!" she exclaimed tightly. "You knew all along he was there, listening to every word I said about him!"

Cole corrected her. "I wasn't listening. I'd just stepped down to the recorder's office a minute to look over some papers and see that the title to my ranch was all in order. You were talking so loud that I could hear you clear down at the end of the corridor."

Crimson flooded her face to the base of her throat where it showed at the neck of the green dress. But this touch of embarrassment did nothing to her anger. She tossed her head scornfully, and put her next speech directly to both the men:

"And what if he did hear? It's just as well! It's best to know where we all stand. I meant exactly what I said. As sure as I'm standing here, I know this man is a rustler. My uncle knew it, and so did everyone else who saw the evidence. And now, if he's returning to this range, I warn you both that the Flying W will be on guard. If he makes one misstep. . . ."

Herb Cole nodded slowly, unruffled, and, shutting the door, came forward until he stood almost a foot above her. There was no humor in his face, nothing but a deadly earnestness: "Frankness is something I admire, Miss Ward. A man can always deal with somebody who speaks his mind, no matter what side of any particular fence they happen to be on. Now me, I'm willin' to return the compliment. The cards I got to show don't amount to much. All I can say is that I've been away for a long time, that there's a lot of work to be done on the Eyeglass, and that I've come back to do it. And if other people leave me alone, I won't bother them."

"Thanks," Betty Ward said coldly.

"As for what happened five years ago"—Cole was quietly looking at her squarely with those disturbing gray eyes of his—"you weren't much more than a kid then, Miss Ward. You couldn't be expected to know directly what it was all about. But I swear to you, I was innocent. All the charges, all the evidence against me, was false. Your uncle. . . ."

She slapped him.

"How dare you!" she flared through lips white and trembling with anger. "My uncle never told a lie, in his life!"

"Wait!" he cried. "Let me finish! I didn't say . . . !"

She was gone while the words were still in his mouth. The door slammed firmly shut behind her, making the wall tremble a little. Herb Cole was left staring with one hand covering the side of his face.

II

The whole room seemed to sting with that slap. Sheriff Duncan had winced in sympathy as he saw it land, and now, into the sudden silence, he let his breath gust out in a windy stream. "Whew," he muttered, "what a temper."

Herb Cole took the hand away from his cheek and looked at his fingers, almost as though he expected to find traces of blood. "Yeah, Tom Ward was her uncle all right," he observed dryly.

"She ain't always like that," the sheriff admitted. "Not more'n a week or so at a time."

Herb Cole shrugged, swung away from the door with stormy thoughts mirrored on his brow. "Does everybody around here hate me as much as that?"

The sheriff stirred uneasily in his chair, then gruffly he admitted: "Well . . . you ain't really popular." He took a battle-scarred pipe from his vest pocket, set it on the desk, got out a plug of rough-cut and a broken-handled knife, and began paring tobacco into the bowl, pushing the blade with one huge, horny thumb. "Some are more broad-minded than others," he went on. "Walt Hubbard of the Bar H, for instance . . . I think you'll find him pretty reasonable. But you better watch out for his foreman, Charlie Moss. Charlie was workin' for Tom Ward five years ago, you'll remember, and he still thinks you're a new brand of pizen. Same goes for Jed Giboney . . . you remember Jed?"

Cole grimaced. "Yeah. That old miser loosened up any?"

"Ain't changed a minute. Rides the same old jug-headed bronc' . . . or its cousin. I can't tell you much for sure about the others, but, frankly, what I've heard didn't sound good."

For a long minute there was silence. As he scraped a match across the desk top, the sheriff sneaked a look at Cole's face and saw the dark, troubled frown that dragged at his mouth. In one corner of the window, a crazy old bluebottle fly was batting itself resolutely against the dusty pane.

"Maybe," Herb Cole said slowly, "it would be better if I didn't try to stay. The West is big, and I did right well for myself ranching below the border. Why don't I drift up to Wyoming or some such place, buy in on a new range where people don't know me and won't lose so much sleep over my movin' in?"

Lew Duncan slammed the point of his knife deeply into the scarred desk. "Don't do it," he growled. "My advice to you, Herb Cole, is stand by your guns and spit right back at 'em."

"Thanks, Lew," Cole said. "That's what I hoped to hear from you. Because the one thing in this world I want is to square myself with my home range, and the folks who live on it. But . . . I just figured I ought to give you a fair chance to speak your mind, if you had any doubts."

The sheriff, puffing at his pipe now, blinked. "Huh?"

"After all, you have no proof that Ward wasn't right about me, just your hunch, and my word, against the evidence. Yet you've risked your reputation, the way you've stood by me . . . keepin' the taxes on my spread paid up with the money I sent from Mexico, lettin' me know all along how things were coming here at home. And if it ever got out how you tipped me off, five years ago, and gave me my chance to make it across the border. . . ."

Lew Duncan's pink bald spot turned a shade pinker. "There's times you have to push the law around a bit, if you aim to come out at the end with something resemblin' justice. I knew you wasn't guilty. I knew that sneak of a Syd Raines

94

was lyin' in his teeth. But Tom was convinced, and, if he'd got you into a courtroom, with his power behind him, you'd have been in back of the bars for a plenty long stretch." He shrugged bulky shoulders. "But now Tom Ward's been dead fer a year. Syd Raines got his a month ago. I didn't see no reason why you shouldn't come back if you wanted to."

"Thanks, Lew," Cole told him soberly. "I hope you'll never regret it."

He took off his gray Stetson, slapped dust from it, gave a hoist to the sagging belt and six-gun that draped his waist. He eyed the sheriff's bent head with a slight gleam of humor touching his mouth. "Just one more thing. I've been meanin' to ask you. What about those hides . . . the re-branded hides they found buried out at my place with Ward's Flying W worked over into my Eyeglass brand. They were the main evidence against me. Funny how they up and disappeared like that."

In his confusion, the sheriff built a quick cloud of pipe smoke about his reddening face. Then he lifted his head and looked squarely at Cole. "Sure funny, all right," he admitted blandly. "They was locked up all the time in a storeroom here at the courthouse, just waitin' a chance for the state to use 'em . . . and I was the only one had a key. But, by golly, one morning they was just gone . . . almost like someone might have taken 'em out and burned 'em, tryin' to cheat the law by destroyin' incriminating evidence. Strangest thing I ever heard."

"Wasn't it though?" Herb Cole met his sly grin. "Sheriff, if I was your official conscience, I'd just about have to give up on you."

As Cole stepped out of the office, the direct blast of the afternoon heat came like the weight of a hand on his shoulders. He didn't mind that. It was part of Arizona—part of the country he loved.

He pulled on his wide-brimmed hat and cast a slow glance up and down the length of the familiar street, noting the changes five years had written across the face of the town. These had been few enough. He was glad it was that way. He was glad to find the place so little different from the way he had left it.

He stepped around the peeled hitch pole in front of the sheriff's door and took the reins of his black horse that had lifted his head in greeting as Cole came out. Putting one hand on the broad space between the intelligent eyes, he patted the bronco gently. "We'll soon be home, Billy. Yes, sir, we're back where we belong."

But he did not swing up into saddle. As he was about to do so, he happened to glance across the street and saw the three men who stood under the wooden awning of the post office, saw their eyes leveled upon him. He knew Walt Hubbard at once. He remembered him as a silent man, one who gave the impression of impartiality in his dealings with others. And there was Charlie Moss, who was now his foreman.

It was the third member of the trio that roused Herb Cole's curiosity. The look of him was instantly familiar. Cole felt that he must have known the man before, yet certainly something about him was very changed. He racked his brains, trying to think what it was and where he had seen that stocky figure, that face with its sleek black hair and trimmed mustache. Was it in Mexico? Or here in Denison?

He looked at the man's clothes, decided he didn't care for the man's taste. The brown cloth suit looked too expensive, the handmade leather boots a bit too ornately turned. Then he shrugged briefly. None of his business.

No point, however, in avoiding a meeting, especially not with Walt Hubbard, the man Sheriff Duncan had told him would probably prove as impartial a judge as he was apt to find among his neighbors. So, trailing Billy's reins over his shoulder, he went across the dusty street. A buckboard and team bearing the Flying W brand were hitched in front of the post office, and he thought briefly of Betty Ward, frowned a little. The girl wasn't in sight.

Now he had reached the other walk and stepped up onto the warped planks. Big Walt Hubbard nodded to him. The other two merely stared, and Cole quickly sensed the open antagonism in Charlie Moss's attitude. The Bar H foreman stood on the step below his boss, eyes squinting at him, thumbs thrust into the armholes of his quill-figured leather vest.

The third man—the one who tantalized Cole's memory so—looked at him with slightly narrowed eyes.

" 'Afternoon," Herb Cole said to them all with a nod that took in the whole trio.

"Hello, Cole," said Hubbard.

The others made no kind of return to the greeting. Herb Cole felt a stirring of anger inside him. He turned his gaze fully on Charlie Moss, nodded again, and repeated through lips that couldn't help tightening a little: "I said 'afternoon, Charlie. Maybeso you didn't hear."

The foreman's perpetual squint screwed a little tighter. His lantern jaw thrust out stubbornly, clamped hard. But Cole was not to be stared down. He gave back better than the other dealt him unyieldingly. A brittle silence lay between them, in the fierce heat of the afternoon.

Perhaps it was the presence of his boss that finally decided Charlie. At last, grudgingly, he gave way. His mouth twisted. He said very shortly: "Howdy." Bit off the word with lips clamped quickly shut, as though he would avoid contaminating his speech by having it touch the man who faced him.

But Cole had won all he needed from the man. He turned

then, looked at the third member of the trio, glanced significantly at Walt Hubbard and back again, a question in his eyes.

The Bar H owner cleared his throat hastily. "Sorry, Cole," he said. "Thought you and Frank knew each other . . . thought he was here at the time you . . . left. This here is Frank Brannon. He owns the B-in-a-Box outfit."

Brannon? A frown tugged at the space between Herb Cole's eyes. And then, all at once, he remembered, but the answer was no less puzzling than the question had been. For the Brannon he recalled was an entirely different sort of person from this carefully groomed dandy. Five years ago there had been a squatter, a low dirt farmer living in a dugout cut into the bank of a stream that ran into Apache Creek, not far from Cole's Eyeglass spread. He had dwelt there all alone, ignored and despised by his neighbors—shiftless, none too clean, surrounded by the rag-tag ends of a two-bit homestead, and by the pigs he raised for a living. Yes! That was it. "Hawg" Brannon was the scornful name the range had called him then. But in the past few years he'd obviously come up in the world. He owned a ranch, Hubbard had said, and with the coming of wealth he'd shaved the stubble from his jaw, exchanged his dirty Levi's for expensive clothing, and, apparently, stepped out in polite society. Why, even Walt Hubbard accepted him now, and called him by his first name. *Wonderful,* Cole thought ironically, *what a little money can do.*

All these things ran through his head as he returned the curt nod the man gave him.

Walt Hubbard, feeling the tension in the air, said in an attempt to ease the situation: "We were just talkin' about heading down to the Irishman's for a drink. Join us, Cole?"

"Sure."

For just the fraction of a second, Charlie Moss balked.

Stiff as a ramrod he stood on the post office step, glowering. His manner said: *I drink with no damned rustler!* But then Hubbard rammed an elbow against his back, hard, and grudgingly the foreman gave in.

Spur rowels scraped and jingled on the scarred planks of the walk as the four of them pushed along in the direction of one of the town's saloons, leaving the murmur of the salt cedars in the heated air behind them. Cole kept to the outside, Billy's reins in his hand. When they came to the wide double doors, he took a moment to anchor the black at the rail handy to a watering trough, then he joined the others, and they went on into the cavernous darkness of the big room.

There were no other customers. At the bar, Hubbard tossed a couple of silver dollars on the polished top and the Irishman set up their orders.

"How's the range holding out?" Cole asked, lowering his empty glass.

"Not too good," Hubbard told him. "Grass is plenty dry, streams are low . . . even for this time of year."

They talked a while about such matters, trying vainly to ease the threat that hung, intangibly, in the air. Brannon and Charlie Moss were doing nothing to help—the latter squinting sullenly at the glass he twisted in his knotted fingers, the other staring moodily at Cole. Cole tried to ignore Brannon's insolent look, but he nevertheless felt the blood growing hot at the back of his neck.

"I'll be wantin' to restock," Cole told the Bar H owner. "I don't suppose I'll find much left on my old range. If you have some feeders for sale, I'll make you a good price for them."

"Fair enough," Hubbard said.

Cole jerked a finger at the bartender. "Another round," he ordered casually.

The Irishman nodded, filled the glasses one by one from

the bar bottle. Brannon's was the last. But as he took Cole's money and started to turn away, the B-in-a-Box owner stopped him.

"Just a minute," Brannon said crisply. "I'm payin' for my own."

He put a coin on the edge of the bar and shoved it forward with the tip of one finger.

Herb Cole felt the weight of all their eyes on him. Even the Irishman behind the counter waited, staring. Cole had already lifted his own glass; he still held it in steady, work-hardened fingers as he turned and spoke to Brannon across the Bar H owner, who was between them. "I said these were on me."

"And I said I was buyin' my own." Brannon's voice was clipped, harsh. "Somehow, whiskey don't agree with me except when it's paid for with honest money."

III

Cole set down his glass carefully. This was inevitable, of course. He had known all along that adjusting to his home range would not be an easy, or a peaceful job. But to have the break come on his first day. . . .

He shot a glance at Charlie Moss, saw that the latter was on the point of refusing his drink, too, following Brannon's lead. He saw the man's mouth open, the words falter on his lips.

But then Hubbard's voice sliced in, stopping his foreman's tongue before he spoke: "Swaller your whiskey and come over here with me a minute, Charlie. I got something I want to talk to you about."

The foreman hesitated, splayed fingers of one hand rubbing uncertainly across the flap of the quill-worked leather vest he wore.

"Hurry up," Hubbard snapped.

Moss gave in. He nodded briefly without looking up, gulped the drink, slamming the glass down on the polished top. Then he and his boss drew quietly away from the bar. Cole and Brannon were left at the mahogany counter, the untouched drinks in front of them.

Cole put his hands on the rim of the bar, pushed away from it, turned slowly, facing the other. It placed his right side and his gun hand free for action, and the space Hubbard had filled lay between him and Brannon. The latter had turned and was facing him squarely.

He jerked a thumb at Brannon's filled glass. "You'd better drink it. Otherwise, I might think you intended something personal by that last remark."

The other nodded shortly. "We wouldn't want to leave anybody in doubt, would we?" He reached, picked up the glass, and for one moment Cole thought the man was going to back down. But then a smirk tugged openly at Brannon's mouth, and calmly he turned the glass end up and poured its contents, in a flashing amber stream, into a brass spittoon at his feet.

Herb Cole's muscles leaped in quick anger. Brannon tossed the empty glass back upon the bar; it rolled across and smashed to the floor on the other side.

"Just who is it you think you're foolin'?" Brannon rapped out. "You and that sheriff . . . do you figure we don't know what you are, what you've been up to the last five years? Duncan says you've been down in Mexico runnin' cattle." Brannon sneered. "Only a damn' fool couldn't savvy what *that* means."

"What does it mean?"

"What it sounds like," Brannon came back. "*Wet* cattle . . . that's the kind you'd deal in. Stolen cattle, pushed across the Río on moonless nights."

"That's not worth answering," Cole retorted. "There's not a word of truth in it."

"I'm not the only one who figures different."

But Herb Cole's look rested on Walt Hubbard as he said: "I know one or two who might be keeping an open mind."

"For how long? Until they see you picking up right where you left off?"

The younger man drew a breath.

Walt Hubbard was watching this scene with a look of growing concern.

Cole, his tone as quiet as before, said to Brannon: "Would you be trying to pick a fight with me?"

"You got the stomach for one?"

It was a challenge. As the big fellow made it, he began a move as if to adjust the neat bolo tie at his throat.

Cole said sharply: "Hold it!" He had the gun from his belt holster as a stride closed the distance between them. His left hand slipped into the gap of Brannon's coat front and re-appeared with a revolver from under the man's arm. "There's what you were reaching for." He made no attempt to keep the scorn from his voice as he re-holstered his own weapon. "I've no stomach for a fight with anyone who wears his gun where I can't see it."

Color flooded the other's face.

Cole drew back a step, moving to place the captured revolver on the bar. He was like this, turned partly away, when without warning a clubbing blow of Brannon's fist smashed into his face, and he was thrown against the bar.

A cry of protest broke from Walt Hubbard. Briefly dazed, Herb Cole got a hand against the bar's edge and shoved himself away from it. Brannon had been slow following up the advantage. Pain, and contempt for a dirty fighter, sent Cole charging at him. Mingled with this was a good deal of the frustration he had confronted, on this long-awaited day of returning. Brannon was big, but Cole had sensed already that he lacked any real skill with his fists. Certainly he was no match for anyone as tough and angry as Herb Cole. The latter tore into him, blocking his opponent's awkward moves while his own fists found their target, again and again.

But the edge of his temper was already beginning to cool; there was little satisfaction, taking advantage of another man's weaknesses. Once, as they broke apart, he heard himself saying: "Look! I can keep this up as long as you can. Call it quits when you've had enough."

Brannon was breathing heavily, almost sobbing with his effort, but he wasn't ready to stop. He kept wading doggedly in, big frame starting to weave uncertainly. Finally, impatient and determined to have the thing over with, Cole set himself and sank a fist, wrist deep, into his opponent's middle. It doubled Brannon over, sent him staggering—for the moment completely helpless. A blow to the hinge of the jaw straightened and drove him backwards. The batwing doors were directly behind him; Brannon's shoulders struck against them, and he went through.

The panels swung wildly. Cole leaned for the man's fallen hat—it was an expensive-looking piece of headgear—and tossed it after its owner. Brannon lay, unmoving, the lower half of his heavy body on the wooden sidewalk, head and torso in the street. The hat skimmed over him and rolled to a stop there, in the dirt.

Already regretting what had happened but knowing he had had no choice, Herb Cole turned back into the saloon. His own Stetson had been lost in the brief fight. He got it off the floor in front of the bar, slapped it against his leg, and pulled it on.

"Sorry," he told the Irishman, and got only a nod in answer. His own drink, that he had paid for, remained untouched. Cole picked it up, but set it down again. He didn't feel like mixing alcohol with his present mood.

Walt Hubbard came over, Charlie Moss trailing him. The Bar H owner didn't look very happy. "It's really too damn' bad that had to happen," he said heavily. "You got a big enough job ahead of you. Something like this won't make it any easier."

"He started it," Herb Cole pointed out. "Refusing the drink, and following it up with fight talk. He would have used that gun, if I hadn't stopped him."

"I know . . . I'm not blaming you. But it was a bad thing, all the same."

Cole was forced to agree; he felt suddenly let down, following the brief adrenalin burst. But now something that had been working at his curiosity made him say: "Brannon seems to have come up in the world since I saw him last. I don't remember him wearing even halfway decent clothes . . . living in a dug-out, with those pigs. What happened, anyway?"

"It was an inheritance. A distant relative in the East somewhere up and died, and I guess the lawyers traced him down as the only surviving kinfolk. Brannon went back there to settle the estate, and, when he showed up here again, he was rolling in money and totally different . . . like you see him now."

Charlie Moss put in with a grunt: "He even *smelled* different."

"Seems kind of funny," Cole said. "You might think he'd want to begin his new life in some other place, where nobody had to know what he'd been before."

Hubbard gave a shrug. "Some people are saying that about a fellow named Herb Cole," he pointed out dryly. "Frank's done all right, though. He bought the old Blackmar place, brought in a crew, and stocked it with good beef. He's won the respect of his neighbors, and it ain't often we remember what he used to be . . . unless somebody like you brings it up."

"The Blackmar place?" Cole echoed. "That puts his graze bordering my Eyeglass spread."

"It does, for a fact." Hubbard looked a little troubled. "He tried to buy Eyeglass . . . claimed it ought to revert to the state, you being a fugitive from justice. But the sheriff wouldn't have any of that, since you'd never been convicted of a crime and somebody or other was keeping the taxes paid up." He hesitated. "I think I better warn you that, over the years, Brannon on the one side and the Wards on the other

105

have been pretty much helping themselves to your grass. After all, with the dry seasons we've been having, there didn't seem much sense letting perfectly good range go wasted. I hope you won't make trouble over it."

Cole's jaw was a little tight, but he shook his head. "I'm not here to make trouble. I just want to get on with my life. I'll give those outfits a reasonable amount of time to move their cattle, and make room for the beef I'll be bringing in. I only hope it won't mean I end up having to impound somebody's livestock."

Walt Hubbard was even more troubled. "Better be damned careful how you handle your neighbors. Betty Ward has public sentiment behind her . . . and, as for Brannon, he's not only got a good-size crew, but a tough foreman to run it for him . . . a fellow named Bat Doran."

"I don't want to make trouble," Herb Cole insisted. "But I have to stand on my rights."

"Of course. I'm just saying. . . ."

Talk was interrupted by a word from Charlie Moss, who had moved over to the batwings where he was looking into the street. He said quickly: "Speak of the devil. Here's Bat Doran, right now."

Charlie stepped aside, and moments later the swing doors were thrust open. A lean, hard-eyed man with a face burned the color of saddle leather strode in, and looked over the room as the panels swung into place behind him. Black, spiky hair showed under a pushed-back sombrero; the fingers of his right hand—long, tapering, their backs matted with black fur—hung close to a holstered gun in what seemed to be an habitual posture. He announced to the room in general: "My boss wants his gun."

It lay on the bar where Herb Cole had placed it when he had disarmed Brannon. The Irishman wordlessly gave the thing a shove. Doran strode over and picked it up. With the weapon in his hand, he turned to put a sharp glance over the faces he confronted, quickly settling on Herb Cole as the only one that was new to him.

"You're the man I'm looking for," he said. "I just want you to know that Brannon is over at the doc's office, getting stitches in the lip you smashed for him." His bold stare raked Herb Cole from his head to his boots. "You must think you're pretty good with your fists . . . but how much do you know about guns?"

It was a challenge. Cole returned the man's stare, above the weapon casually pointed in his direction. He said shortly: "I guess I know which end the bullets come out."

A slow grin warped the other's mouth. "Very good," Doran said, nodding in mocking approval. "We're gonna be neighbors, I understand. Maybe it'll work out for me to give you a few lessons."

"If it comes to that," Herb Cole replied, his tone devoid of emotion, "I expect to be ready."

Suddenly Walt Hubbard blew up. "Damn it, this talk about guns ain't getting us anywhere! Every one of us has better things that need doing."

A moment longer Bat Doran held his stare on the man from below the border, the weapon still loosely held, then he gave a shrug as he shoved it behind his waistband. He turned to the door, but with one hand hooked over a batwing panel he paused and looked back for a final shot. To Herb Cole he said: "You ever heard of the statute of limitations?"

"What about it?"

"Oh, nothin' much. Only . . . accordin' to that law, you let a man possess and make use of your property for a period of three years without lodging protest, and it ain't your property any longer. It belongs to him." He chuckled, a little harshly.

"You been away *five* years, ain't you? Mister, by that statute you ain't got no ranch any more."

Herb Cole's fists knotted tight. "I know nothing about law," he retorted. "But I do know this. I'm hereby giving Hawg Brannon three days to start cleaning B-in-a-Box cattle off Eyeglass and back onto his own grass. You tell him that."

The other chuckled again. "I will," he said pleasantly. With a quick, lithe movement, he stabbed the batwings open and slipped through, leaving them to beat the empty air as he moved quickly out of sight.

For a long moment there was no sound. Then Herb Cole dragged a deep breath, and turned to the other men.

Charlie Moss shook his head. "I swear, that guy gives me the creeps. I ain't sayin' I've changed my mind about you, Cole," he added with a frowning glance at the man from below the border, "but I sure wouldn't enjoy being in your boots. I'll have to wish you luck with someone like Bat Doran."

Herb Cole placed a hand on the old man's shoulder. "Thank you for that, Charlie," he said earnestly. "And I won't stop hoping I'll be able to change your mind before this is over."

"I'll be hoping that myself," Walt Hubbard put in. "Personally I'm for any man in a tight . . . at least until he convinces me, beyond any reasonable doubt, that he's guilty. And somehow I don't think that's going to happen in your case. In fact, I'm counting on it."

On that note, they parted.

IV

On the street again, Cole stood a moment under the saloon arcade, debating. Now that he was back, impatience was in him to take the lonely trail out to his Eyeglass spread—to make some tangible step in the tremendous job of rebuilding and re-adjustment that awaited him. He was tired, physically and spiritually, from the long miles he had ridden since dawn, and the battle with Brannon, and the exhausting encounters he had already experienced. But as he stood there, he checked over in his mind any further business he might need to attend to while he was still in town. He decided there was nothing more to hold him.

Until he had checked at Eyeglass, he could not judge what supplies he would need to order, although they would certainly be many. Meanwhile, there were trail rations in his saddlebags—food supplies to last him a day or so, when he would in all likelihood be making a buckboard trip in and doing some large scale stocking-up.

He went to where Billy waited for him in the tie pole lineup, and was jerking loose the knot in the reins when Lew Duncan came hurrying along the plank sidewalk, panting his name.

The sheriff came to him—a disheveled and bareheaded figure, blue eyes staring in wild excitement. "My God, fellow!" he cried hoarsely. "I didn't expect to find you alive. Somebody tracked me home and told me you'd beat up Frank Brannon, and that his foreman was out to smoke you down for it. What the devil have you been up to?"

Cole shook his head. "I haven't done so good for a start, have I . . . trying to make friends for myself? But at least I'm getting a clear idea who some of my enemies are, and that's something."

Putting up a hand, the sheriff ran it across his bald spot in a habitual gesture; he was plainly distressed. "Boy, if I'd known it would be this way . . ."—he faltered—"if I'd guessed they'd have such a hornet's nest primed and waiting for you, I . . . I dunno that I'd have suggested this. You was doin' all right in Mexico."

"I'll go back, Lew," the younger man said quickly, solemnly, "if you say the word. I don't want to make it rough for you by staying. But . . . I don't *want* to go."

"Then don't." The sheriff's eye lighted, his jaw set firmly. "Stick it out, and give 'em hell. And . . . good luck to you."

Cole said: "Thanks, Lew. Those are almost the same words Walt Hubbard used. If I've got men like you two on my side . . . or at least willing to hold back judgment and give me a chance . . . then that's plenty to ask. And I promise you, I won't let you down."

He swung tiredly to saddle, and lifted a hand in farewell as he put Billy away from the hitch pole and pointed him northward along the trail, snaking past the drab adobe hovels, across the tawny range toward far vermilion cliffs. The sheriff was still standing there, watching, the last time he glanced behind him at the shimmering dust of the town.

There had been no further sign of Bat Doran although Cole kept a sharp eye out for him. He had no illusions about Dorn. He had the man pegged as a dangerous opponent, indeed—more dangerous and probably a good deal more intelligent than Brannon himself. The B-in-a-Box owner was a vain and stupid sort of man, a threat only insofar as his wealth could buy him the services of one like Dorn, and the location of his ranch holdings placed him contiguous to Cole's Eyeglass graze.

Doran's talk about the statute of limitations had him worried more than he cared to admit. He didn't know too much about legal technicalities. He ought to have taken the thing up with Sheriff Duncan and seen what the lawman had to say about it. But his jaw hardened. B-in-a-Box still had just the three days he named to show what their intentions were as to moving their stock off his grass. Then he would move—although he wasn't yet sure just what step he would take.

But another thought struck him that he didn't like. Betty Ward's Flying W beef were also on his grass. She would have to receive the same treatment as the encroaching neighbor on his other flank. She was a snippy, hot-headed little person for all her good looks. She was, in short, the niece of old Tom Ward, and he had no business letting her like or dislike of him make too great a difference.

So his crowded thoughts ran on, as Billy took him at an easy gait across the rolling ranges to the ranch he had not seen in half a decade, to what would always, for him, be home. Nostalgia and an eager impatience clotted his throat as the well-remembered country unfolded itself. It seemed that he remembered every twist and turn of the lazy wagon trail, every butte and mesa that cut the paling sky on the horizon, every new, far vista that the twenty miles unfolded to him.

The sun was losing a little of its fierce heat now, as it dragged down the western sky and turned coppery, its light running with a new golden quality in these last hours before the end of day. But its effects were evident, all about him—in the brown slopes of the range, in the dry arroyos that had been rushing streams before the rains failed and summer's heat turned their muddy bottoms to barren, flaking stretches of cracked adobe. Even Apache Creek, when he crossed it at the fording, was low, sandbars showing above the sluggish surface.

111

It had been a dry season, all right, and not the first. But these things went in cycles. The rains would come, even to this part of Arizona; the range would green out again; cattle would fatten on the rolling acres of rich grass. But until then, feed for hungry stock would exert a powerful pressure on the ranchers. It wouldn't add any to the welcome they would show Herb Cole, coming back just at this time to put more beef—his own—onto graze his neighbors had been appropriating. He had to remember that.

At the head of a deep arroyo the road forked, one branch angling eastward into the wash, another crossing it and pointing north, a third bending in a broad arc toward the sunset. That way lay the huge Flying W holdings of Betty Ward, and the smaller spreads that fringed it—Hubbard's Bar H, the Frying Pan, and a couple others. The arroyo trail led toward the old Blackmar Ranch, which was now Brannon's B-in-a-Box; a smaller branch of this would take you also to Jed Giboney's Horseshoe layout, and finally to a scattering of nester spreads along a remote stretch of Apache Creek.

Cole sat saddle for a moment, letting the map of the region lay itself out in his mind, getting reoriented. He could fit his own Eyeglass graze into that mental map—well-watered, rolling acres, breaking against the foothills and the vermilion cliffs to the north, hemmed in by the two big outfits that were helping themselves to his grass.

Then he sent Billy down into the dry arroyo and up the steep yonder bank, and over the little-used middle fork of the trail. Excitement lifted in him as he found himself upon his own graze, his own earth. He saw cattle, bearing a variety of brands—mostly Ward and Brannon stock. Nowhere was there an Eyeglass steer on this range where once his small, but good-blooded herds had run. He was prepared for this. Lew

112

Duncan had warned him of how, five years ago, his crew had left when Cole himself was forced to take flight into Mexico, how the stock had gone untended, the increase running unbranded and turning into mavericks that had finally received his neighbors' various brands, the remnants of his herds finally drifting into the foothills when B-in-a-Box and Flying W shoved their own stock onto Eyeglass range. Probably some of them were still to be found, running wild back there under the rim, gaunted and savage after years of such existence. It would be a heartbreaking job to try and chouse them out of that brush.

With these thoughts Herb Cole rode northward through the last hours of afternoon, and sunset colors were rioting in the sky when he skirted a long, low hogback and saw before him the log and adobe buildings, the mesquite pole corrals of the home ranch. As he reined in for a long look, he was struck bitterly by the desolate, friendless atmosphere that hung upon the deserted place. It seemed a symbol of the bleak prospect presented by his own return to this country. He spoke to Billy, and rode on down to the house.

The place was as desolate as he expected to find it. Weeds choked the yard between the buildings; the corral poles were down; at one corner the roof of the feed barn had fallen in. Cole dismounted, a heavy feeling pulling at him as he moved about the place that had been his home.

He saw that everything was just as it had been that day when the crew had hastily abandoned the ranch, on hearing that their boss was wanted by the law and had taken his flight to Mexico. The door to the bunkhouse hung open on a broken hinge. Range varmints had been having a field day here, amid the litter that had been left behind and deep drifts of sand and silt deposited by rain and wind. The three-room house itself looked to be in better shape. He saw no sign of looters—although there would have been little enough to tempt them. Face down on a table next to his leather easy chair he spotted the book he had been reading on the fatal evening when his world fell apart. He picked it up and glanced at the title page, put it down again. On the desk were tally books and letters, dust-covered. In the tiny bedroom his bunk was rumpled and unmade, just the way he had left it. A few articles of clothing still hung from nails in the closet.

Everything in the kitchen would need a thorough going over before he could fix another meal here. Luckily he found a tin that still held a fair amount of kerosene. After a cleaning and refill, the lamps would give him light to start cleaning up the mess.

Plenty to be done, and little time for reminiscence. Herb Cole went outside again to his waiting horse, stripped him of saddlebags and gear. He had to replace the fallen poles of the corral before he could turn Billy into it. By this time the last color had died in the west and gray dusk was settling across the land.

In the kitchen, lamplight now lay warm and mellow, softening the neglected look of the place, rendering it almost home-like. Cole had to grub out a lot of dirt, however, before he could use the kitchen to prepare himself a meal.

He grabbed a water pail and stepped out to fill it at a never-failing spring that bubbled from a rise above the house. The young night sky was a rich, deep blue above dark, sharp outlines of building and rock and bush. A single star burned white in the west. Framed there in the oblong of yellow lamplight that the door put at his back, Herb Cole felt the sudden slap of concussion as a rifle bullet streaked past and clapped into the wall behind him.

The shot laid its roar upon the stillness, battering away to echoes. Cole, throwing aside the metal pail, was leaping quickly out of the band of light, going to one knee on the hard earth as he sought its covering shadow. Crouched there, keening the night, he waited for another shot, but none came. Either the ambusher thought his first one had done the trick, or was reluctant to fire a second time and expose his position.

Impossible to place the location of the rifle exactly, from his uncertain recollection of its startling sound, but he thought it must be up there somewhere on the hill behind the house. There, a watcher could command the lighted door and windows of the kitchen with an excellent vantage point and good cover.

Herb Cole slid his long-barreled Colt from holster and held it, letting it rest against his thigh. There had been no sound of a horse going away. This made him think the bush-whacker was lying low, waiting for some telltale sign that would reveal whether the first bullet had taken effect or not. If somebody wanted him out of the way badly enough to lay an ambush for him, they probably wouldn't give up until they were sure they had succeeded.

A muscle in his bent leg began to cramp and to ease it he straightened slowly to his feet—froze that way suddenly. Somewhere in the thickening darkness a mesquite twig had snapped under the weight of a boot with an explosive sound. Turning his head slowly, Cole searched out a wide arc of shadow, foot by foot, but could see nothing at all. Then, yonder near the barn, something moved in the night and Billy stamped uneasily in the nearby corral.

Cole flipped up his gun and thumbed off a shot, the violent sound of it reverberating against the wall beside him, its flash tearing at the night. Instantly he was changing position, and, when an answering bullet came seconds later, it drilled the air exactly where he had stood when he fired. Aiming at the flash, he plugged a second slug toward the corner of the barn and was at once running forward, determined to bring this to a showdown.

His assailant, whoever it was, didn't wait to face him. Cole saw the dim patch that a light-colored shirt made against the night, moving hastily away. Before he could raise a target on it, the ambusher had ducked behind the corral, and, with the frightened Billy stomping and bucking in there, Cole didn't dare to risk a shot. He ran forward with redoubled speed and, reaching the bars, turned along them to the closest corner.

Pulling up then, he heard the running horse—starting somewhere near at hand, and drumming away quickly into the night. The ambusher had found things getting too hot for him and was clearing out, his job left undone. Very quickly all sound of him faded out to nothing, and it was not even possible to tell, in that wide darkness where sounds bounced back and forth among the rolling slants and rock faces, in what direction he had ridden.

Herb Cole leaned shoulders back against the corral poles, letting the strengthening night breeze fan against his lean and scowling face. Billy came mincingly to thrust his head through the bars, nuzzle his sleeve in search of sympathy. Herb Cole hardly noticed.

"Now, who?" he muttered angrily, and thought he could manage a fair guess. Not Flying W—he somehow couldn't let himself believe that Betty Ward, however sharp her temper and however great her hatred of the man who had been her uncle's enemy, would have conceived or condoned such a method of eliminating him. The only alternative was Brannon, or his foreman—and Bat Doran would not have to sneak about in the night to put a bushwhack bullet into him.

He shook his head. "Hawg Brannon is more worked up over my coming back here than I imagined. At least he hasn't wasted any time."

Grimly, as he pondered, he jacked the spent shells from his gun and fumbled new loads from the canvas loops of his belt. There was, of course, no hope of tracking the unsuccessful ambusher. Tomorrow, maybe, he would be able to locate sign up there on the hill that would help point to the ambusher's identity. Nothing to do about it tonight—except take greater precautions and make sure no further attempt on his life might find him as unprepared and open to a bullet.

Back at the house, he hung blankets across the windows and felt better when he was thus protected from spying eyes. There wasn't any further disturbance, however. He took his pail to the spring and filled it, not hearing any alien sound above the normal night noises. He fixed a meal from his trail rations, bolted it hungrily. Satisfied he was not due for further visitors, he made up his bed in the long-empty bunk.

But he kept his six-gun handy, in the blankets, and despite exhaustion slept with his mind close to the surface, ready for an attack that never came.

V

Next morning he saddled Billy and rode up on the hill to check for sign. With a trained eye he quickly spotted what little there was—where a horse had been tied in the brush, and where the ambusher had hunkered down to watch the ranch below. He even discovered the bright copper casing of a Winchester bullet, jacked from a rifle's breech after the shot. But that was about all.

The boot tracks that he located, leading down to the barn and the corral and then, at a dead run, wide-spaced, back to the tied horse, showed nothing as to the man's identity. When he followed the trail of the mount, it quickly played out on hardpan north of Eyeglass headquarters. He rode back to breakfast, still certain in his own mind that Brannon had been behind the shooting but knowing it was not a thing he could prove.

He spent most of the morning checking further at headquarters, making notes on the work that had to be done, the necessary building repairs, the supplies most urgently needed. On closer inspection he saw that looters had been at work during his long absence—a thing, after all, to be expected. Drifting riders probably had gone over the place from time to time, removing anything that appealed to them, destroying wantonly. They had left the house pretty much alone for some reason, but they had been through the barn and stripped it of every scrap of extra harness he had stored there as well as his farm wagon and even a half barrel of horseshoe nails. When he went the twenty miles into town that afternoon to make his first purchases, he would have to ride Billy, and hire a wagon and team at the livery in Denison to haul his plunder back to the ranch.

When he arrived in town, there was little activity. He saw only one person he knew—the old man at the stable who fitted him up with rig and team. The streets were empty, and, when he pulled up in front of the mercantile and went into the cool interior, fragrant with its mingled odors of leather goods and bolted cloth and tobacco and coffee, he discovered that the proprietor was new to Denison since his time. The man knew who he was, however, and his curiosity and suspicion were only half concealed.

Cole thought of telling Sheriff Duncan about the attempt on his life, but quickly decided against it. There was nothing the law could go on, and, moreover, he meant to stomp his own snakes and not bother the officer who had already taken on so much unnecessary trouble on his account. So he stayed clear of the courthouse. In the Mexican quarter at the edge of town he arranged for a woman to come out next day and clean up the house and bunkshack, then, handling the team and with Billy following the wagon on a whale line, he rolled slowly back to Eyeglass.

That night there were no visitors, with or without guns.

Awakening at gray dawn, he lay a moment in the blankets of his bunk, wondering what it was that had roused him. He heard no sound, no movement, but there was something very definitely strange, and then, as his senses cleared, he realized what it was. Someone was brewing coffee.

He came out of the bunk reaching for his pants, shoved his legs into them, and slipped his gun out from under the pillow. Jerking up the belt with one hand, he carried the gun at his side as he padded, barefooted and shirtless, across the bedroom and silently worked the knob of the door, cracked it open.

Gray light lay upon the untidy litter of the long main

room. There was no sign of anyone, but the tantalizing coffee smell that had leaked in around his door was stronger here—and then, from the direction of the kitchen, came the definite sound of a chair creaking under the shift of a body's weight. Carefully Cole eased through the bedroom door, put his shoulders to the wall, and went cat-footing along it with the gun leveled, his bare feet making no sound on the rough puncheon flooring. Lamplight glimmered past the open kitchen door. He slid up to the jamb of the door, put a cautious look around its edge.

Herb Cole didn't think he had made any sound, but now faded blue eyes lifted and speared him there in the doorway. Ignoring the gun in Cole's fist, his visitor's hard mouth twisted into a grin; gaps showed blackly among the discolored teeth. "Hi, sonny!"

Cole lowered the gun and moved through the doorway. His astonishment was plain. "Niobrara! What are you doing here?"

"What does it look like? I'm brewin' java. A couple cups of this Arbuckle of yours, boiled black, should put stren'th enough in my carcass while I fry up a half dozen eggs and a side of that fresh pork rib I seen in the cooler yonder. Don't mind me borrowin' your vittles, I hope? Ain't had a right decent meal lately."

"Of course, I don't mind . . . help yourself. But . . . I thought I left you down in Sonora. I figured it wasn't safe for you right now, up this side of the border."

Niobrara Jones lifted bony shoulders in a shrug, inside the oversize coat he wore. "Ran into a little trouble down there . . . had to carve up a captain of *rurales* who didn't favor the shipment of *carabinas* he caught me bringing in by mule train one moonless night. I figured I was a mite hotter on that side than I was up here . . . seein' as I've been out of the pic-

ture for a spell, far as these *gringo* badge toters are concerned.
So I took me a *pasear* to greener pastures."

He got up, slouched across to the stove, and lifted the lid
of the big iron pot and sniffed blissfully at the cloud of steam
that puffed out of it into his face. "Pret' near ready," he murmured. Like a man thoroughly at home, he went to the box
cupboard, took a couple of china cups off their hooks, blew
dust out of them, and set them on the table. "Join me?" he invited.

"Sure." Herb Cole drew back a chair opposite Niobrara's,
sat down, laying his gun aside. The coffee the gunrunner
poured for him was boiling hot and stout enough to make a
man blink, but Niobrara drained two cups of it in quick succession and almost as many breaths. He ran a sleeve across
his mouth then, and looked at the younger man.

"So this is the Eyeglass you used to tell me about, huh?"

"How did you find it?"

The outlaw shrugged. "Findin' it was no problem. I knew
close enough where it would lay. How you makin' out, sonny?
Your face looks kind of bruised up. Been fightin' somebody,
maybe?"

"Seems like I've been fighting ever since I reached home,"
Cole admitted. He had swallowed down all he could of the
terrible coffee, and he pushed the half empty cup back, stood
up. "There's nobody I'd rather talk to about it," he said, "but
let me drag the rest of my clothes on and get some breakfast
thrown together first. A man can parley better over a full
stomach and a smoke."

The wicked, slitted eyes appraised him shrewdly. The
gap-toothed mouth stretched in a grin. "Sure thing, sonny.
I'm your hairpin. Do you have trouble to talk over? Trouble's
my given name." Stubbing a quirly butt into the leavings of

fried egg and wheat cake and bacon rind upon his plate, Niobrara went on: "So it comes down to this. Five years ago, somebody was workin' a long loop overtime on Flyin' W beef. Old man Ward got proddy. Bein' scared of him, and needin' a goat, this somebody rigged up a frame and fitted you into it. You hightailed. The rustling come to a halt. And . . . less than a year later a gent we shall call Hawg Brannon shows up all of a sudden loaded with gravy. An inheritance, he says."

Herb Cole shook his head wearily. "It looks peculiar, I'll warrant, and it's had me doing some hard thinking along just those lines. But if Brannon had the brains it would take to pull a slick frame-up, what was he doing living in the dirt with a mess of pigs?"

The outlaw shrugged. "A front," he said. "The stakes he was aiming for, he could afford to play that kind of a part. But this inheritance business . . . it's just too much to swallow. One thing sure. Whoever it was framed you, it's someone who's still right here on this range . . . one of your neighbors. If it was some fly-by-night rustler, he needn't have gone to all the trouble to find a scapegoat and throw suspicion off himself. He'd simply have pulled stakes and vamoosed when operations got too risky. No, just think it over. And who else would it be, if it ain't your hog-lovin' friend?"

Herb Cole considered the argument. "I just don't see it. Brannon's a loud-mouthed troublemaker, and that's about all. The foreman he hired to run his ranch for him has twice as much brains . . . and is twice as dangerous. I could believe some such notion about Bat Doran . . . not about Hawg Brannon."

"But didn't you tell me, you guessed he tried to 'bush you night before last?"

"I'd whipped him in a saloon fight. It would be like him to want to get me for that."

122

The outlaw shrugged again, and pushed back from the table. "I'm only suggesting how it looks to a guy on the outside . . . a guy that's been pushed around some, and done his share of pushin'. As you say, I don't know any of those people. Maybe, when I've had a chance to run my eye over the cast of characters, I'll be able to come up with something better."

Cole looked at him, surprised. "You planning to be in the neighborhood a while?"

Niobrara hesitated. He actually looked a little embarrassed. "Tell you the truth, I thought I might hole up *here* a few days . . . if it wouldn't bother you too much, havin' a reprobate like me around. That bunkhouse out back don't look in too good a shape, but I reckon I can clear enough space to unlash my bedroll."

"You're more than welcome. Though I ought to warn you, the sheriff here, Lew Duncan, is nobody's fool."

"You don't need to worry," the outlaw assured him. "I ain't hankering to meet no badge toters. Mainly I'm up here for rest and quiet, while those Mexican *rurales* have time to cool down a little. But I ain't forgettin', either, the night in that Ciudad *cantina,* and the half-breed who'd have slipped his blade between my ribs . . . if only a locoed son named Cole hadn't barged in to help another *Americano* out of a tight."

The younger man colored a trifle. "All right, all right," he said gruffly. "We won't talk about that. But . . . I'm really glad to see you here."

VI

Cole saddled and they headed north across Eyeglass range. Niobrara's mount was an ugly brute. Niobrara did everything but kick it in the jaw to settle it down. But Herb Cole knew the beast must have speed and endurance or the outlaw wouldn't have been riding it.

The morning was as warm as those that had come before. A high overcast had moved in from beyond the vermilion rim, and it hung like a film across the brassy sky but did nothing to lessen the smash of the sun. Niobrara Jones, squinting at it, said: "Might rain." He sounded dubious.

They rode at an easy gait across the rolling grass. This was good range because the proximity of the rim meant gently tilting acres cut by a generous pattern of watercourses. Even in a dry year, these and the natural springs that bubbled up from the base of the rim kept Eyeglass green and well grassed, and it was not surprising that, in his absence, Cole's neighbors should have encroached farther and farther upon his range until, between them, they had loaded it with their stock.

Beyond, where rolling grass slants broke against the foot of the steep, eroded rim, were the tangled roughs and steep arroyos where the remnants of his own herds probably could be found, running wild. Cole's face went a little hard as their jaunt brought them in view of more and more scattered bunches of cattle, all bearing the Ward Flying W and Brannon's B-in-a-Box.

He had told Niobrara about the deadline he had laid down. "Guess I lost my head," he admitted, thinking about it. "I can't hope to enforce an order like that without a crew.

Yet, come tomorrow, if nothing's been done to move their cattle off, I'll have to make some kind of gesture, or lose face. Dunno what I was thinking, to have let myself get backed into such a corner."

"Worry about it tomorrow," Niobrara said indifferently. "This kind of a game, you gotta talk tough to hold your own. Everybody on either side of you . . . both this Brannon character and the Ward girl, who sounds like a nice-lookin' filly but a real spitfire . . . the whole works of 'em is out to see you don't get you a toehold back here and take over the grass they've been usin', free of charge. Don't let 'em fool you a minute! That's the real stake they're fightin' for. All the talk about old rustling charges is no more'n a danged smoke screen."

"Maybe you're right," Cole agreed darkly. "What about this statute of limitations thing, Niobrara? You reckon they have a weapon there?"

"The devil with it!" the outlaw snarled, hard mouth lifted above snaggled teeth. "A six-gun is gonna hold this graze, sonny . . . no damn' law in no book!"

Herb Cole considered this grim pronouncement as they rode across the bunch grass range under the waning morning. The rim was close enough that they could see the shadowed ravines that broke its eroded scarp.

"Full of holes as a sieve, ain't it?" the outlaw remarked suddenly. "You ain't said it, but I bet a cookie that, when the rustlers were operating, they shoved their stolen stock right up those ravines, across your north range, and over the rim."

"That's correct," Herb Cole admitted. "It's wild country, flinty and not taking much trail. Get a bunch of beef critters up there, and a rustler could run them in any direction . . . even double back and hit for the border, if he was so minded, by aiming for the bad country eastward around the nester settlements and the head of Apache Creek, and south that way. Roundabout, sure, but not too long a drive for one night if they kept pushing the cattle right along."

"You had this figured out?" the other demanded, looking at him. "And yet you couldn't stop them?"

Cole shrugged. "Too much rough territory to keep a watch on all of it. We tried . . . even formed an organization and kept patrols riding the breaks. But they were naturally spread pretty thin, and it wasn't hard for rustlers to get past them. At any rate, plenty of cattle disappeared on moonless nights, without us ever catching a rustler in the act. The trails were always stone cold when we found them, and they soon lost themselves in the rimrock."

Niobrara tugged at an earlobe, his ugly face twisted in thought. "Might be worthwhile to have a look up there."

"You can," the younger man grunted. "I've scouted that country till I'm sick of it. I'm gonna take a saddle count and get a line on just how many head of foreign stock I'll have to shove off my range . . . or impound."

Three quarters of an hour later, Herb Cole was resting his saddler in the scant shade of a fringe of piñons near the western edge of his graze, when he heard cattle coming down the throat of a draw below him, moving west. There was the scuff of hoofs in rubble, the lowing mutter of the animals, then, distinctly, he caught the faint cry of a rider yelling at a slow-moving critter to hurry it. Cole had been fashioning a smoke but he quickly scattered the tobacco, shoved the rice paper into a shirt pocket, and then shifted in the saddle, pulling his gun belt around so that the walnut grip was ready to his hand.

The first of the cattle appeared, then—a red-white shape, moving through the leaf shadows dappling the bottom of the draw. Others followed in a lazy flow, heads down, tails swishing. Cole saw the dark burn on each bony flank—Flying W. Ward cattle. Moving westward toward the invisible boundary line that separated the larger spread from his own.

Betty Ward wasn't waiting for a deadline! Her cattle were leaving his graze.

A steeple-hatted rider came into view now, shouting and chousing the cattle through the draw, a coiled rope spinning in his hand. Another crowded close behind him through the slanting bars of shadow and the dust haze, and, as he recognized this figure, Herb was quickly kneeing Billy forward, down the sharp pitch of the slope, out of the trees.

The girl saw him and reined about, and the cattle ran on and the dust settled as she waited for him. She was dressed boy-like in jeans and boots and a loose blouse that didn't conceal her slender figure. A broad-brimmed hat hung between her shoulders from its leather neck thong, the black curls free and wind-ruffled and glinting brightly under the sun.

She looked flushed and very pretty, indeed—it amused him a little to think back in a flash of memory to the gangling, awkward kid she had been when he had left, five years ago—but there was no pleasure in the stare with which she greeted him as he slid Billy down the stony bank of the draw, and pulled rein, finger at hat brim.

"Well," she said without preliminaries and with a coldness of tone that chilled his momentary feeling of friendliness, "we're pulling them off . . . but you don't need to flatter yourself that I'm scared of you. I just know what a temptation it is, having other people's cattle where you can lay hands on them!"

For a moment he could only stare. Then his jaw went hard with ridged muscle showing white beneath the tan. "You never pull in your claws, do you? Maybe you'll tell me how I'd go about rustling your cattle, single-handed?"

"Oh," she answered archly, "I daresay you've got a whole picked crew of border jumpers, probably holed up somewhere on top of the rim. The way you were threatening Frank, he says you must have been pretty sure of all the help you needed."

The accusation was so preposterous that for a moment he couldn't be sure he had heard right. He battled to keep a hold on his slipping temper.

"Dear Frank says that, does he?" he lashed back at her sarcastically, pointing up her use of the man's first name. "Anything he says sits OK with you, I reckon. The two of you must be pretty thick."

She colored. "Mister Brannon," she retorted, correcting herself, "is my neighbor and an honorable man. We have interests in common . . . why shouldn't I listen to what he says, and work with him to protect those interests? I heard all about the fight you picked with him in town . . . the way you mauled him, until he needed three stitches taken in his cheek. It just confirmed my impression of the kind of man you are."

"I see. Did you by any chance ask Walt Hubbard or Charlie Moss to give you their version of that fight, and of what started it?"

From the way she hesitated, her glance wavering, he knew he had scored a point. But, woman-like, she wasn't going to admit it. She looked away with a toss of her head. "I don't want to talk about it any more. Will you let me go now? There's a lot of beef to be moved across to Flying W graze, and gathered for shipment as soon as I can arrange a drive to the railroad. I haven't grass enough to feed them for more than a few days at the most."

She lifted the reins and would have ridden on, but Billy was crowded close against the flank of her roan and Herb

Cole wouldn't give ground. He said in a flat, cold tone: "You've no use for me . . . *bueno!* But let me warn you. When I fight, I fight for keeps. And though I don't like to fight a woman, that won't stop me if you and your friend Brannon start crowding me too hard. A friend tried to warn me, not more'n a couple hours ago, that that's just what the pair of you were up to . . . to be rid of me and keep Eyeglass for yourselves. I didn't want to believe it, but I can tell you right now that if he happens to be right. . . ."

Her breast lifted, fury flaming in her eyes. Next moment Herb Cole had to throw up an arm and catch her wrist in strong fingers, as her open palm came swinging at his face. "You are the slappingest female!" he exclaimed. "I don't seem to know how to talk to you without setting you off!" As she jerked her hand free, he went on in a different tone: "But I do want to thank you for moving this beef, without making me ask you. I'd prefer to stay on good terms with the Flying W, if it's at all possible."

Her eyes held his for a moment longer, with nothing in them but anger. Abruptly, then, Betty Ward jerked the reins and sent her little mare down the draw, away from him. For a second time Herb Cole was left staring after her. After a moment, with a shake of the head, he turned Billy in another direction, hardly aware just then where he was riding.

VII

His mood didn't improve, and he sought to work it off by hard riding and steady saddle work. Eyeglass was a big expanse of graze, with a lot of up and down to it. Herb Cole figured he should make an inspection of his range—to check on the condition of the grass and the water sources, and familiarize himself with the whole sprawling domain—before venturing on the major step of restocking and hiring a crew to help him manage it.

The job was one that could have used up the heart of two days easily, and Herb Cole set about completing it in one. These preliminaries were holding him back, turning him impatient, keeping him from the active job of starting his spread on the road to a rebirth of what it had once been. So he drove ahead, under the high sun and the haze across the sky that never came to more than that and only seemed to press the heat back upon the land.

The sweat trickled beneatht he brim of his wide hat, stained his shirt in damp circles beneath the armpits as he put Billy to the slants and hollows, working from point to point on his tour of inspection. He pushed the black harder than he should have, but Billy was game and stood up under the tough regimen.

Finally, taking pity on himself and his horse, Herb Cole halted for a spell of rest, slipping the bit and loosening the cinches so that Billy could graze with comfort. He broke out some meat sandwiches he had brought along in his saddlebags, and made a belated lunch of them. As he ate, he wondered what Niobrara Jones was finding to interest him up in the rimrock to the north. There had been no further sign of his reprobate outlaw friend, and Cole concluded he must still be up there somewhere, scouting that high, broken badlands country.

In his riding, he saw that there was a good deal more Brannon cattle on his range than there was of the beef carrying Betty Ward's Flying W iron. He also noticed with a grim interest that Frank Brannon was making no move as yet to start removal of his beef. Unlike the girl, he was choosing deliberately to ignore the deadline. That put the next move squarely up to Cole.

Toward four o'clock, with sunlight a golden patina across the wide land and shadows lying barred and long, Cole rested a second time in the shade, Billy tearing at the grass somewhere at his back. In a moment they would be starting on the long haul to headquarters. Cole had swung eastward as far as the dry creekbed that marked the boundary between his own land and Brannon's. He had done some mental calculating, and tomorrow he would see Walt Hubbard concerning the stockers they had talked about. He would arrange for delivery of the cattle to his ranch as soon as he could hire a hand or two to help work the start of his new herd.

A boot step crunching dry earth was the first warning that he was not alone. He looked up and saw Frank Brannon standing with a six-shooter pointed straight at him. He also saw the court plaster now covering the split lip Cole's fist had given him.

He might have made a reckless move to his own gun, if it hadn't been for the voice that warned sharply: "Better not!"

Still seated, Herb Cole quickly turned his head. Bat Doran and another man—a big, tow-headed cowpuncher with the look of a Swede—had him flanked from that direction. They had come silently and caught him flat, and there was nothing he could do about it.

131

He eased carefully to his feet, trying to sidle around so he could watch all three of the men, but the blond giant moved with him and blocked that. Now Brannon paced closer, his injured mouth scowling under its bandage.

"Take his gun, Nels," he ordered.

Cole felt it leave the holster, heard a brief crackling of brush, and then a *thud* as it was tossed aside. He waited, facing Brannon; when the man spoke, the damaged lip evidently gave him trouble forming his words.

"We got things to settle!" His voice was literally shaking with anger. "You think you can come back here, set a deadline, tell me I got to give up grass I been using the past four years. But then, by God, to go and tear my face up for me . . . !"

The outburst suddenly made his priorities clear. Along with his wealth it sounded as if Hawg Brannon had acquired, all at once, a regard for personal appearance—not only in his wardrobe but, if the neatly trimmed mustache was any indication, what he seemed to think of as his good looks. In his woolly thinking, the idea that someone's fists could have disfigured him seemed to have grown to an obsession, overnight.

Cole answered him bluntly. "Anyone who can't take a few bruises, shouldn't go around picking fights."

The man didn't like that at all; his face flooded with color. Bat Doran said, in a tone that held little regard for his employer's feelings: "You're letting him ride you, Frank."

"And he's gonna be damned sorry!" To the yellow-haired giant looming over the prisoner Brannon gave a curt order, then: "Grab his arms, Nels. Hold him steady."

Before Cole could make a move, both elbows were seized and yanked together behind his back, rendering him helpless. Brannon closed on him. The man had put away his gun. He shoved his left fist under the prisoner's jaw to force his head up while he flexed the thick fingers of his other hand, the fist

132

opening and closing while a hot stare traveled the other's face to choose a target. Cole understood, then, what was about to happen to him. At the last moment he suddenly let his whole weight drop forward in the grip that held him, as he violently jerked his head aside. The strike of Brannon's fist did no more than graze him, and send his hat flying.

That brought a roar of fury. To Nels, Brannon shouted: "Damn it, I said *hold* him!"

The man responded. This time, Cole almost thought his arms would be torn from their sockets. As he was hoisted to his feet, Brannon roughly trapped a fistful of his victim's hair, while his other hand brought up the gun from its holster. He jammed the muzzle fiercely against a cheek bone. What he read then in the face directly above his own made Herb Cole's breathing clog in his throat.

Then Bat Doran spoke. "That's enough," he said quietly. "Go on any further with this, and you'll end up killing him."

Brannon muttered something that sounded like: "Good riddance!"

"You're wrong there. If he was to be found dead, you can figure who that sheriff friend of his would come looking for. You'd better want this fellow kept alive. It's just lucky you missed the shot you took at him, two nights ago. I won't tell you again. Lay off!"

Cole almost thought the big fellow was beyond hearing, but something seemed to have registered. Slowly the bunched shoulder muscles eased; thick fingers released their grip on the prisoner's hair, administering a painful twist as they let go, but in the next breath the barrel of Brannon's gun rose and came chopping down again, hard. To Cole it was as if his head had exploded. He dropped into nothingness.

When he awoke, it was to a darkness that was nearly complete. He lay with pain, stirring a little as consciousness returned. He tried to sit up, groaned, and again went limp to the throb inside his head.

In the blackness around him he could not think at first where he was. He looked up then, and saw the mesh of stars stretched across a deep sky and knew that night had come upon the world as he lay there. A moon hung halfway up the sky. He must have been lying here for hours.

He was aware of movement somewhere nearby. He pushed up from the hard ground, searching. He heard the rattle of a bit chain, the stomp of a hoof. "Billy!" he said. The black, all but invisible in the night, came up to him and a cold, wet muzzle touched his cheek.

He had been left lying where he had fallen, battered Stetson beside him. He picked this up, but his head didn't feel as if it wanted him to try putting it on just yet. With a groan he managed to make it to his feet. He did appear to show improvement moment by moment. Now he remembered his gun that Nels had tossed aside, and was determined to find it. It cost him an effort. Working blindly, prowling through the thick brush and kicking at it with his boots, he luckily came across the weapon, leaned for it without falling over, and returned it to his holster.

All this time he believed his head was clearing. Now, as he thought over that encounter with B-in-a-Box, one idea came through clearly and somehow it stuck in his mind. A strange set-up, there. Woolly-headed as Hawg Brannon might be, he seemed to have enough respect for his foreman to listen to his advice and even be led by him. Still more remarkable, some tersely spoken words by Doran had been accepted as if they were orders—almost a reversal in the rôles of owner and employee.

Billy had been grazing and was rested, ready for work. The

blow from a gun barrel had settled to a dull throbbing, but it left Cole with an overpowering thirst. He pulled himself into the saddle and, having got his bearings in the chill evening, set a course for the nearest fresh-water stream.

Dismounting there, he knelt and drank deeply, afterward dashing cold water on his face and head. He felt better instantly, his thoughts and senses clearing. He stood there by the singing water, waiting for Billy to satisfy himself. The night was wide and silent under the stars, the contours of the earth strongly etched in moonlight.

The black having finished, Cole swung up and pushed on across the sandy bed of the stream, up the farther bank. It was not until he headed a rise beyond that he caught the first hint of movement in the night. He almost dismissed what he had heard as a mistake on his part when a shift of the wind against his face brought it again—a brief rumble of hoofs against earth.

It was swept away again immediately, but now Cole was sure. He spoke to Billy and sent him lunging down the slant, toward a jumble of broken country ahead. The black was sure-footed and eager to run, and his rider gave him his head until he saw the dark scar of a ravine cutting across the moon-bright spread of land in front of him. At its edge he pulled rein, as the sound of moving cattle came to him stronger than ever. From his saddle, Cole could make out a tide of dark shapes flowing through the cut below, almost thought he caught the sheen of tossing horns. Distinctly there came the lowing protests of beef cattle being driven.

There was no legitimate reason why cattle should be moving across his range, especially at this hour of night. He saw they were starting to thin out, as the main body of the drive passed him. And now he saw riders—he counted three of them, working the drag. The wind brought a sound of voices, yelling at the stragglers. Voices of men who spoke in Spanish.

He urged the black forward. Billy hesitated at the edge of the drop, but, like the good cow pony he was, he started down, picking his way with care. It was a six-foot drop; they slid for the last half the distance. At the bottom the dust made a pungent haze all about them, kicked up by the horses and cattle. Cole's belt gun was in his hand as he sent Billy after them, up a slight incline toward the rim that he knew would be rising somewhere ahead.

Sounds of the drive grew quickly louder. Almost before he expected it, he came in sight of the stragglers and at once made out the shapes of the riders. They became aware of him at almost the same moment. Someone yelled out—again, in Spanish. A pistol shot came at him, a streak of flame and flat gun sound.

He never heard the bullet. He brought up his own revolver and threw off three quick shots, trying for each of the three in turn. Unbelievably, in that kind of shooting, one appeared to find a target. There was a cry of agony such as a badly hurt man makes, and a rider was swept from the saddle.

The hammer of his Colt fell on an empty chamber. Then, all at once, Billy was fighting the bit—he had never had a gun go off so close to his sensitive ears. Cole spoke to settle the horse, while he cleared the cylinder and dug fresh cartridges from his belt. By now the last of the stolen cattle had moved out of sight, but the riders were still there and at their job of covering the rear. Their weapons streaked muzzle flame, not scoring. Billy had never faced anything like this. He was fighting the bit as Cole tried to hold him in and return the fire—and then the gun hammer fell on a spent cartridge.

His horse out of control and an empty weapon in his hand, he suddenly had no choice but to retreat. Pulling the black in

136

by sheer force, Cole got him turned and headed for a scatter of boulders he had passed just moments before. He left the saddle and threw himself into this protection.

Billy, let loose on trailing reins, for once forgot his range training. Goaded by terror, he turned and bolted back down the ravine. His owner yelled at him; he paid no heed, and was quickly swallowed up in the night. Herb Cole had to let him go. He could only hope that, once over his fright, the dragging leathers would bring the black to a halt and stop him from running far.

He was working to reload his gun when a bullet slapped into the boulder beside him and ricocheted with a high scream. One of those people out there had a rifle! Cole hadn't thought of bringing his Winchester with him today, never imagining he would need it. With his revolver only partially reloaded, he hugged the protection of his boulder while he tried to locate where the rifle was firing from. It spoke again. He saw the muzzle flame, and at once threw off a couple of shots from his handgun, hoping without much confidence that it would keep the rifleman pinned down while he made up his mind what to do next.

One rider down, a second one yonder with a high-powered saddle gun—but, where was the third? Gone ahead, to catch up with the rest of their crew and bring help? Again the rifle sent a bullet to *spang* against the steep bank of the ravine behind him. Cole ducked involuntarily, wishing again for his own Winchester as he clutched his handgun and the wind whipped the sting of powder smoke into his face.

Then, above and behind him, a sound of iron striking against stone brought his head around. Too late, he saw what had happened to the third Mexican. The man had put his cayuse up the bank of the ravine and now was almost on top of Cole's position there in the boulders. The cowman quickly saw himself utterly exposed.

Without having time to reload, he spun away from the boulder that had now become a futile shield, and, as he did, a bullet from above just missed nailing him—and the firing pin of his own gun fell once more on an empty chamber.

VIII

He did an ignominious thing—the only thing open to him. He turned and ran back down the ravine, slipping and falling and scrambling over the tricky footing. Just above him the rustler drove his horse along the bank, yelling taunting jeers in Spanish as he sent bullet after bullet at the fugitive. In that poor light, with both of them in motion, a hit was unlikely, but the Mexican's mocking laughter sounded confident enough.

Clutching an empty six-gun, Herb Cole fled from that laughter and from the slam of lead into the rocks about him. Suddenly one high-heeled boot turned on loose rubble and he felt himself going down, to hit the ground in a sprawl at the same instant that his pursuer fired again.

Half stunned, he lay as he had fallen, something warning him not to make a move. He could only hope the other man would think his last shot had dropped him. No! The weapon spoke one more time, lead striking near enough to spatter him with chips of rock as his very gut seemed to knot tightly. But that was the end of it. Apparently satisfied he was dead, the Mexican on the bank of the ravine had turned his horse and was pounding away again. Night finally swallowed up the sound and stillness fell.

Herb Cole stirred, and shakily pushed himself up. He found he was drenched with sweat, and the night wind lanced through him. His first move was to load his gun, noting as he did that more than half the loops of his shell belt were now empty. He was running seriously low of ammunition. He was thinking about that as he got to his feet, and set out to find his horse.

It seemed like an hour that he worked his way down that

ravine, his rider's boots making awkward going of it, but at last he caught up with Billy, standing, motionless, with his dangling leathers trapped in thorny brush. The black was still shaken and glad to be found. He nuzzled his owner's chest as Cole stroked him, scolding him for running away but not putting much heat into it—a horse that had never experienced gunfire could hardly be blamed for spooking when he did. Convinced that he was finally settled, Cole told him— "We still have work to do."—and reached for the stirrup.

That was when he really felt it. Waves of weakness swept through him; the pain in his head, from Hawg Brannon's pistol whipping, was throbbing again, so that he had to grasp the saddle horn and lean against Billy to keep his feet under him. It eased finally, but it was a warning that he was pressing his limits. He tried again and this time made the saddle. He fought against the pain in his head, telling his horse: "Let's take it easy, now." He turned Billy again in the direction of the vanished herd.

To his ears, a strange stillness lay over this broken country. The wind had fallen, and there was little more than the occasional scrape of Billy's irons on rock, the creak of saddle leather. When he came upon the site of the brief gun battle, there was no hint of it, nor any sign that one of the rustlers had been wounded or maybe killed. He must have been picked up by his companions and taken on with them.

Cole pulled up and sat with his two hands on the saddle horn, bracing himself, and peered in the wake of the vanished herd with the high shape of the rim lifting before him into moonlight. He felt that he still had some reserves left, and he sent Billy ahead.

The course of the ravine was growing steeper, making the horse work a little harder. Still there was no sound of anything moving ahead of him, no hint of raised dust in the still air. Cole knew from this that he had been left far behind. Suddenly, without any warning, the high *spang* of a rifle whipped across the stillness. He pulled rein sharply, even though he knew that sound had come from a considerable distance, possibly miles.

Although he waited through long minutes, the shot wasn't repeated. Whoever fired it and for whatever reason, it probably had nothing to do with him, but it put a sharp edge on his caution as he spoke to Billy and sent him ahead.

Some minutes later, he drew up and left the horse on grounded reins while he climbed to a point where he could have a wide view of this region. Far below, the range country spread in folds of moon-frosted grass with an occasional sparkle of water and, away off, the scattered lights of a ranch building or two. Ahead, the rim was empty with no hint of a living thing other than the brush. A nighthawk swooped suddenly close to him, and was gone on silent wings.

Herb Cole was thinking that it was just as it had been five years ago—the sudden strike of cattle thieves, the disappearance into thin air, the trail too cold to follow. This apparently had ceased during the years he was gone. Now, just two days after his return to Eyeglass, it was all beginning again, almost as though some evil fate dogged his footsteps.

The night was getting old, the moon dragging down toward the west. Cole returned to his horse, again feeling the drain on his strength from that blow with Brannon's gun barrel. He pulled his shoulders back and lifted the rein. Billy, too, had had a long day. Cole said: "Let's go home."

The hour was well past midnight when weary man and bronco trailed into the home ranch. The place was dead silent. Seeing no horse in the corral, Herb Cole thought for the first time in several hours of the old outlaw, Niobrara. He stripped the gear from Billy and turned him into the pen, slung the heavy stock saddle on the top pole, and spread out the sweaty blanket where the air could get to it.

The bunkhouse door was closed. Cole shoved it open, looked about in the moonlight that slanted through the windows. "Niobrara?" he called. He could see, though, that the long, low-ceilinged room was empty. A half-formed thought was running elusively through Cole's mind, vanishing before he could put a finger on it. He was in no shape just now to hunt after it.

In the house he found that the Mexican woman from town had been there in his absence, and seemed to have done a good job of cleaning the place. It looked almost home-like, as yellow lamplight chased the shadows back into the corners. But any pride of possession was swamped by other emotions just then. He threw together something to eat from odd scraps he found in the kitchen. When he piled into his bunk, exhaustion poured its black waters upon him, and the dull, continuing ache within his skull gradually receded and left him.

Once again he awoke to the aroma of coffee brewing, but this time he knew what it meant. He lay a while with eyes still closed, sending out feelers that didn't immediately find evidence of the sickness that had plagued him since the blow from Hawg Brannon's gun. Finally opening his eyes, he dropped his feet over the edge of the bunk and levered himself to a sitting position. There were no fireworks in his skull, so Herb Cole rose and dressed and got into his boots. He swung his gun belt into place then, and went to see how matters stood in the kitchen.

Niobrara Jones sat just as he had the morning before, scowling at the contents of his coffee mug. He showed the same stubble of whiskers; his narrow eyes were bleary and bloodshot—his general haggard appearance, that of a man who needs a good night's sleep and hasn't had it. As Herb Cole entered the kitchen, the nod of greeting he got was curt and perfunctory.

"You're late risin'," the old man growled. "Sun's nigh an hour old."

As a matter of fact, it lay on the eastern horizon as if resting there; its level rays came through the window and spread a warm golden patch across the table covering. Herb Cole took hold of the chair across from the outlaw and pulled it out, but didn't sit. He stood there, one hand on the chair back, and watched as Niobrara indulged in a jaw-splitting yawn, scrubbing his mop of mouse-colored hair with one blunt hand.

"Haven't been to bed yet, have you?" Cole observed

He spoke mildly, but something must have crept into his voice. In the middle of the yawn, slitted eyes shot a glance that speared the younger man. "No I ain't. For a fact." He watched Cole with that keen stare.

The half-formed thought that had plagued Cole the night before came to him now in full force, sweeping over him with a chill suspicion. He put it in brief words, and not pulling his punches. "Did you really come up from Sonora alone . . . or did you bring some of your border-jumping friends with you, looking for the chance at something good for yourselves, maybe?"

The expression on the outlaw's face turned cold and hard as graven stone. "Keep talkin'," he snapped.

There was danger in every line of him as he sat there looking at Cole. Over on the wood range, the coffee pot boiled unnoticed.

The younger man still had his hand on the chair back,

making no movement toward his own belt gun. "I ran into some cattle thieves last night, running stock across the rim. I didn't see any of their faces, but I heard their talk. Mex voices. Made me think of you, Niobrara. I think you know what I'm getting at. You and your outfit have run more than guns across the border on many a moonless night. Now you come up here, uninvited, and you get awful interested in that hole-in-the-wall rim country. And last night you were so busy at something or other you never did make it to bed."

An oath tore from the lips of the outlaw. Niobrara came up from his chair to lean across the table. His ugly face thrust at Cole, his narrow eyes glittering, he spat his words. "You're callin' me something close to a liar, sonny. An' you better be careful . . . I just might forget what happened in Ciudad."

"What were you doing last night?" Cole demanded, not faltering before the naked danger of the other man.

"None of your damn' business!" Niobrara's glittering stare cut to the six-gun at Cole's waist suggestively. "I'm through talkin' to you, as of right now. If you feel like pullin' a gun, just go ahead . . . I'll accommodate you, by Gawd. Otherwise, you and me got no further business." His mouth twisted. "Uninvited, you said! You needn't've added another word. Me, I'm walking outta here . . . right now. You're welcome to your lousy java . . . and your busted ranch, and the guys who are tryin' to run you off of it. You couldn't beg me to stay a minute longer."

He turned his back and tramped stiffly from the room, a loose-hung, stooped man who walked with a sidling, crabwise motion, the ludicrous outsize coat he wore effectively concealing a brace of deadly weapons.

Through the window Cole watched as the outlaw moved through sunlight to his ugly, iron-jawed bronco that drooped by the watering trough. Niobrara took his shapeless hat from the saddle horn and jammed it on, then swung adroitly to the stirrup and into the saddle. He kicked the vicious horse to set it moving. Without a backward glance he went riding from the Eyeglass yard.

A feeling of depression settled on Herb Cole as he turned from the window, with the last sound of the horse threading out in the still morning. He had handled that very badly. If he was mistaken about Niobrara, then he had wronged a man who, for all his lawlessness and unscrupulous nature, had in his own way been trying to serve him as a friend. And if he was right? Now he wouldn't have the old outlaw where he might have been able to keep an eye on him. Either way, he was aware of a sudden real sense of loneliness as the coffee pot drew his attention, and he went to move it off the fire.

IX

Later, Herb Cole hitched the team to the borrowed livery stable rig, and headed for town with Billy following at the end of a whale line—today was Saturday, and there was a good chance of running into Walt Hubbard with whom he had business to discuss.

It looked like another scorcher in the making. Dust devils walked across the far-rolling ranges where the tawny wagon road looped. Heat waves shimmered off the adobes of the town, and the salt cedars above the post office made only the faintest movement in the nearly lifeless air.

Several broncos ranged the tie rack in front of the tin-arcaded building. This was unusual, he thought, but he supposed the mail coach that served the town twice a week from the nearest railroad was expected in shortly. There would be no mail on it for Herb Cole. He turned into a side street and drove his rented rig into the wagon yard next to the public livery.

He didn't see the old man who ran the place, but he had paid in advance so he wrapped the reins around the brake handle and, mounting Billy, rode away and left the team and wagon standing there. On the main street he saw that the mail stage had just pulled in. The postmaster, in sleeve supporters and green eyeshade, stood in the street to catch the pouch the yahoo tossed down without slackening his teams. Cole didn't go down to the post office. Instead, he dismounted in front of the Irishman's, shoved through the swinging doors, and walked inside.

There was no other customer. The Irishman was sweeping the floor down with sawdust as Cole entered. He canted his broom against a table and moved around behind the bar to fetch out the bar bottle and pour the drink Cole asked for. The latter could see him peering closely at his face, but the man made no comment. His greeting was pleasant enough, although Cole thought he detected a note of something behind it.

He took the drink and waved away a second one. He looked at the backbar where the customary slate with piece of chalk attached by a string served the range as a general bulletin board. It was empty of writing at the moment.

Cole indicated the slate with a jab of thumb. "I'd like to post a notice," he said. "Eyeglass is looking for riders."

Without comment, the Irishman reached him the slate, and Cole chalked his message, stating the wages he would pay. He was not much of a hand at writing and this took a little time. By the time he finished, the Irishman had gone back to his sweeping, so Cole went around behind the bar, set the slate in place against the mirror. He said: "I'll be needin' some hands as soon as I've put through a deal with Walt Hubbard for feeder stock. I'd appreciate it if you'd do what you can to kind of push this thing."

The man halted his work, leaned on the broom as he gave Cole a direct look. "Sure. But maybe you better not set up nights waiting."

"No?"

"Not many would think it was a lot of fun, signing on with the Eyeglass right now."

"It's that way, huh?" Cole had known it would be. He came around the counter, scowling as he prodded the saloon man further. "A bad reputation?"

"A dangerous one," the other amended. "Jobs are easy enough to get, that grub-line riders don't have to pick one with the promise of hot lead mixed in it. And the wages you're offerin' ain't the kind to attract professional gun handlers."

"I don't want gun slicks," Cole said flatly. "Eyeglass is an honest spread, and it's not going to be pushed into a range war if there's any chance of keeping from it."

The Irishman shrugged. "I wish you luck," he said dryly. He watched as Herb Cole turned toward the batwings. It must have been some instinct of friendliness that prompted him, at the last moment, to add a warning: "Better walk sharp! I think Jed Giboney's still in town."

Cole turned back slowly. "Giboney? What about him?"

The other's broad face turned quickly expressionless. "Guess I spoke out of turn," he answered. "Thought maybe you'd heard what he's yelling around this morning. If not, you better find out from him. I carry no tales."

He bent to his sweeping, and Cole knew there would be nothing further to be learned here. Frowning, and with a presentiment of danger, he turned and pushed out of the saloon into the breathless blast of nearing noon.

Although the mail coach had already come and gone, the crowd in front of the post office had not thinned out any, but after what the Irishman had told him, the scene yonder held a new significance for Herb Cole. He was aware now of excited talk, carrying to him along the half block distance. He went to his bronco, ripped the reins free from the tie rack, but he hesitated a moment before lifting into saddle, a frown of uncertainty on him.

He had no desire to mingle in that group yonder—especially not if, as he more than half suspected now, he was himself the subject of their excited talk. On the other hand, he couldn't run away from a scene, however unpleasant. If there was trouble, it might be better to face it out—clear the atmosphere.

Then he spotted Walt Hubbard's stocky figure, and this

decided him. After all, his next business was with Hubbard, concerning the feeders the Bar H boss had agreed to sell him.

He started down the dust strip, leading Billy.

They saw him when he was almost upon them. At once, voices sheared off, heads turned to stare at him. He saw Charlie Moss in his ever-present quill-worked vest. He saw Sheriff Lew Duncan with a package of Reward dodgers under his arm—a package just off the mail coach, he supposed. He saw other men he remembered from the old days, a half dozen of them.

Only one of the lot had not fallen silent as Cole moved up, and in the stillness his crabbed, piping voice carried loudly. "You'd be yellin', too, if it'd been you that lost fifty head last night! Don't worry, you'll all have your turn. There ain't nobody immune. He got away with it five years ago, and he figures he can do it again."

Someone said tensely: "Watch it, Jed."

The speaker, cut off by the warning, turned uncertainly to throw an anxious, squinting glance around him, looked squarely at Herb Cole, and passed him over unseeingly although they were only a dozen feet apart. Jed Giboney was notoriously near-sighted—and too damned stingy, his neighbors had always figured, to squander his money on a pair of glasses. He was small, scrawny, dried-up, with stringy gray hair he kept pushed back under a greasy hat.

He didn't look like the owner of a spread the size of the Horseshoe, but that's what he was—a mean-spirited, penny-pinching little man who had grown even drier and skinnier in the years Cole had spent in Mexico. Now his watery blue eyes had found their focus on the face of the newcomer. Head thrust forward, he squinted at Cole and for a moment—a moment only—was at a loss for speech. He dragged a deep breath into his chicken-breasted body. "You!" he screeched.

"After last night, you have the gall to show your face?"

Cole dropped Billy's reins, looked around him at the silent group, not liking what he read from their manner. To the sheriff he said: "What is it I'm supposed to have done now?"

Lew Duncan told him: "Giboney says some of his cattle were run off last night . . . fifty head or more. This morning one of his riders found they were gone and followed the tracks across your range and up toward the rim until he was sure. I'll be going out directly to have a look myself."

"Does he think I rustled fifty head of beef, single-handed?"

"How do we know how large a crew you got stowed away somewhere?" old Giboney retorted. "Only back two days, and already picking up where you left off." He turned his anger on Lew Duncan. "You still don't see it? And yet you call yourself a sheriff."

The lawman met his look with stolid patience. He refused to raise his own voice. "I call myself a sheriff because people like you elected me to wear the badge. I serve it as best I can, with my limitations, and I take a single step at a time. Only after I see what I find, up at the rim, will I be ready to take the next one. I get hoarse sometimes, trying to tell people to keep an open mind, until there's a good reason for shutting it." He turned to Herb Cole. "You could help, if you were to stay more or less out of the way for a while. Some people seem to get short-tempered just seeing you around. No sense in deliberately riling them, if it ain't necessary."

Cole replied evenly: "I'm in town on legitimate business with Walt Hubbard. After it's taken care of, I'll be glad to leave. I ain't in the business of riling people. Should the law need me, for anything at all, I'll be at Eyeglass. I got plenty there to keep me busy."

Lew Duncan thanked him with a nod, and turned back to

the others. As he did so, Hubbard himself appeared at Cole's elbow to say: "I'm available right now. Let's talk."

It was not easy to turn away from an open challenge, or from the suspicions Jed Giboney had all too clearly been rousing here, but Cole felt obligated to help the sheriff any way he could. He took Billy's reins again, and the two cowmen moved a short distance along the street, where they halted to discuss their business. They needed only a few minutes, having already settled a price between them; Cole reported the number of head of feeder stock he had decided on, and Hubbard promised they would be ready for him to check over before putting down his money. Actual delivery at Eyeglass would wait on his hiring a hand or two to help with them.

As soon as they had shaken on the deal, Herb Cole swung into saddle, willing enough to leave the town to its peace. But he had no more than pointed Billy in the direction of Eyeglass when a sudden drum of hoofs sounded behind him, and a harsh voice was shouting: "Cole! You wait up a damn' minute!"

He looked over his shoulder, then brought Billy around as Charlie Moss came tearing up on a big, rangy gray, his quill-worked vest flapping. Pulling to a dust-scattering halt, the old fellow laid his voice into the quiet of the morning and he didn't tone it down any. "Something I want to make clear, mister!"

"Charlie!"

Walt Hubbard, standing in the gray's settling dust, spoke sharply but for once his foreman wasn't to be interfered with. "Stay out of this, Walt!" His eyes bored into the man in the other saddle. "What I got to say don't concern Bar H. I'm talkin' now about Betty Ward."

Cole's mouth hardened. "This is no place to discuss. . . ."

"I ain't discussin'!" Charlie's lantern jaw shot forward. "I'm *tellin'* you, mister! I used to ride for the Flyin' W, and I don't intend to see harm come to Betty because of some grudge you might still be holdin', account of your differences with Tom. She had nothing to do with that. Right now, she's putting together a shippin' herd, on the flats west of your graze . . . cattle that's been pulled off Eyeglass in the last couple of days, rather than have trouble with you. And I'm givin' warning. If anything happens to that herd, I'll be comin' after you, personal! You got that straight?"

The words whipped across the waiting silence of the street. It took Herb Cole a moment to gather his control so he could answer.

"Charlie," he said quietly, "you're one tough old bird and I could never be mad at you . . . even if you are as bad as Jed Giboney for getting a notion stuck in your head where dynamite can't dislodge it. Because I also never knew a man who could remain faithful to a brand he once rode for, even if he no longer worked there. Someday, if I'm lucky, I might hope to see someone like you on *my* payroll. I mean it."

He touched a finger to his hat brim in salute, and turned away, leaving Charlie Moss staring after him with a look of baffled anger. Lifting the reins, Cole glanced along the street and only now noticed Bat Doran beneath the overhang in front of the Irishman's, lounging there as his black-matted fingers shaped a cigarette. Their eyes met, a cold look passing between them. Doran turned and said something to the pair standing beside him—one was the yellow-haired Swede, Nels, the other, a nondescript cowpuncher who was obviously another of his B-in-a-Box crew. Whatever their boss had said, it sent them into snickering laughter. Cole was almost certain the remark had to do with him and, perhaps, Betty Ward. But he had given Lew Duncan his word about not starting any trouble, and he had to swallow his anger. He noticed that Doran had taken no part in the laugh. The man's eyes remained cold and probing as the three of them watched Herb Cole deliberately turn away, to give the spur to Billy.

A little north of Dennison, Cole halted in the shade of a tall cottonwood and dismounted, letting the horse graze, while he found a seat on a fallen limb to think over every moment of that business in town. He found very little to encourage him. Presently he spotted a lift of dust from the road. He was mounted and waiting when Lew Duncan approached him at a canter. He ranged the black alongside the sheriff's mount. He said: "I was waiting for you."

"I dunno why," the sheriff grunted. "Nothing further I can tell you."

"But *I* have something you need to know, that I didn't feel like discussing in front of that crowd, especially not Jed Giboney." As they rode on, he continued: "I was there last night. That's right . . . I had a run-in myself with the ones who stole Jed's beef, though I didn't know whose it was at the time. We traded some lead."

The sheriff was staring at him. "Is this on the level?"

"God's truth. Now you know why I was waiting to talk to you."

As they continued riding, Cole laid out full details of the encounter, clear to the point where he had been forced to turn back—he said nothing about the blow from Frank Brannon's gun barrel that had been the main reason for that, only that the trail had become hopelessly lost to him. "Like I said, I had no way to tell whose cattle were being raided . . . only that they had no business crossing my grass."

Duncan was scowling ferociously over all this. He wanted to know: "How many do you think it would it take to move fifty head and keep them together, at night?"

"In that country? It's hard to say. All I ran into was the three riding drag. I managed to nail one of those, I don't know how badly. One thing, though, is kind of interesting. They all talked Spanish."

That got him a look. "You figure them for Mexicans?"

Cole nodded, but the sheriff added thoughtfully: "Of course, most of us *gringos,* here along the border, can handle the lingo."

"Sure . . . when we need to. Hardly ever among ourselves . . . like you and me right now."

Lew Duncan acknowledged that with a nod. Suddenly he gave a soft whistle as something occurred to him. "Now that I think about it, it's just as well Jed Giboney doesn't know this. He'd be saying, for sure, those were people you brung up here with you to help in your deviltry."

The other nodded. "And now you see why I only told *you.*"

Duncan rubbed a palm over the bristles on his jaw. "Anything else you think of, that I ought to know?"

Herb Cole was caught up short, as he realized he had nearly forgotten Niobrara Jones. A renegade and a smuggler, scornful of any law on either side of the border—knowing all the routes for moving stolen goods, and no doubt with plenty of every breed and nationality ready, on call, to take his orders. If the sheriff knew someone like that was loose hereabouts, he could hardly overlook him as the most obvious suspect.

And yet Cole held his tongue. Bleakly he determined that for now this had to remain between Jones and himself. If the man had imposed on his hospitality, pretending friendship and gratitude because of that incident at Ciudad—and then betrayed him with a rustling for which he would be sure to take the blame—one way or another that was something he would have to settle personally. As long as there was any doubt remaining, he balked at setting the law against someone who might not be guilty. Especially someone for whom he must admit an odd but very definite liking. So he said: "No, I wouldn't say I can think of anything just now."

They fell into silence. The scud of hoof beats in dust took over the noontime stillness as the range fell behind and the vermilion rim drew nearer through a haze of heated air. They dipped toward Apache Creek, and halted to water their horses at the crossing.

Lew Duncan said: "Whatever happened last night, it can only make your job that much harder. In time, people might forget that old trouble . . . but they can't overlook a sudden, new outbreak. Meanwhile, I've heard talk about B-in-a-Box using the statute of limitations to claim your grass that they've been using. I wish I knowed more'n I do about the legality of that, but if there is something there, looks to me your best chance of fighting it is to show you were hounded out of the country five years ago on an unproved accusation. If you were innocent, and it was beyond your power during those years to protect your range from being encroached on . . . well, I'd like to think an honest judge would have to agree with you."

"I'd like to think so, too. Looks like it's squarely up to me to try and keep the peace . . . if I possibly can."

"Well, I got to be trackin'," Duncan said. "Got a trail to find."

The other suggested: "I can save you some time . . . take you directly to the spot where I ran into trouble with those Mexicans. You can start from there."

Duncan thought about it, but shook his head. "That might look kind of funny. We've already arranged that Giboney's rider will show me the sign he picked up. I better stay with the

155

plan. Anyway, those animals made it to the rim hours ago. Up there, not much chance of finding them . . . too many ways to lose a trail, or hide the critters before setting out for markets no one but a thief knows about."

"Or swinging south with them to the desert and Mexico," Herb Cole added.

"Whatever. . . . Actually I figure I'm only going through the motions, to try and convince Jed the law respects his interests. Not that I think he'd ever really believe it."

With that Duncan nodded in farewell as he put his sorrel down the eastern branch of the wagon road, into the throat of a rocky wash that led to Jed Giboney's Horseshoe spread.

Herb Cole sat for some time watching his dust as it spiraled and melted away against the sky. Afterward, he took the middle branch of the fork, and pushed on toward the lonely work awaiting him at Eyeglass.

X

The sun rolled higher above the empty range, tipped a little over toward the west. The looping, dusty wagon road lay empty. Once in a great while a rider put his bronco along it with a plume of dust straining the air behind him and slowly settling. A hawk wheeled across the sky, wings spread and motionless, pivoting gracefully on every slight current of air until it swung from sight beyond the north rim. For a long time after that, there was no movement.

Then an old, stoop-shouldered man came north along the trail, hunched in the battered saddle with bony legs doubled and feet shoved into stirrups that were short enough to accommodate a boy. His bronco was a gaunt bone bag. It had a spine-cracking gait as it shuffled through the dust, but the rider evidently meant to stick it out and ride that nag until it dropped, getting every last mile out of it before he would use another.

When he came to the Apache Creek crossing, the horse wanted to linger for a drink, but the old man jerked up its head sharply, not even letting it snatch a mouthful of the cool water as it went through. From his fierce scowl, it was plain that boiling anger rode with him and that he had no thought or patience for anything else with that roweling mood upon him.

Clop of shoe iron against stone announced the approach of the old man on the bony horse, threading a jogging course down this arroyo trail that led eastward from the forks toward B-in-a-Box, Horseshoe, and the nester settlement. He came into sight around a twist of the arroyo floor, and the man beside the trail waited until the rider was almost on top of him before he said sharply: "Hold up!"

Jed Giboney hauled rein with a convulsive jerk of gnarled fingers, a gusty exclamation breaking from him. "Who is it? What do you want?" Head thrust forward, he sent a hurried, questing glance about him. His near-sighted eyes could not find the speaker for a moment, and then they made him out, dimly, a faceless outline.

It stood before him without movement, without answering. A first touch of fear began to crawl through the old man and he repeated, with a trace of panic: "Who is it?"

The man on the ground laughed at him. "It don't matter who I am." His voice held something familiar, although perhaps an effort was being made to disguise it. "But *you*, you damned trouble-maker! You've made your last fuss! This is the curtain on the final act." And there was the sound of a gun, going to full cock.

"What do you . . . ? No! Wait! Oh, my God . . . !"

All of a sudden, terror had the old man in its grip. His blinking eyes strained to make out that dim, blurred outline, or were there *two* of them?

"Got any prayers, you old goat?"

Suddenly Jed Giboney remembered he was on a horse— his enemy, whoever it was, grounded. With a frenzied flailing of skinny legs in shortened stirrups, he tried to kick the nag into a gallop, to take him past this danger. But his own parsimonious nature now proved his undoing. The old bone heap had no gallop left in it. It made a pathetic lurch forward. The other man laughed again.

Giboney's half-blind and watery eyes caught the gleam of a gun barrel. His screech lifted into the heated air, bleating out the identity that had flashed upon him in that last, dread moment. "No! No, Cole! Herb Cole . . . don't!"

The blast of a revolver ripped through his words. The old

man jerked and went twisting out of saddle; the weary nag drummed ahead with stirrups flying as it left its master there, dying in the dust.

There was a *vega* on Eyeglass range of good grass and well watered by a never-failing seep spring, which Herb Cole had kept under wire for a segregation point in his constant efforts to breed up his small herds. In five years the three-strand fence had broken down, the poles rotting out in some places and in others obviously having been pulled out by mounted men with ropes.

Cole had worked there all that afternoon with post-hole digger and axe—resetting poles, chopping out new ones from a nearby mesquite thicket. He had wire on order at the general store, and, when it came, he would rent a wire stretcher from Walt Hubbard and do the job of restringing. Now, sweated out and tired, he tightened Billy's cinches and swung astride, returned to headquarters with the sun low before him above the western hills.

He rode into the musty silence of the barn, left the black standing in harness while he unlashed his fence-building tools, and stowed them away. The axe head had come loose and it fell off as he started to rack the tool on its pegs. He was looking around on the shadowy dirt floor to discover where the head had gone when the noise of the horses came to him across the ranch quiet.

From the volume of sound, and the rapidity with which it grew, he could guess there were quite a few horsemen and that they were coming fast. The knowledge held something ominous. Cole left the axe handle leaning against a post and went out the wide doorway of the barn, unconsciously giving his gun belt a hitch. He stood there with arms akimbo, a feeling of trouble tightening in him as he squinted against the blaze of setting sun on the southwest horizon.

They came in a knot of black figures, fanning out as they neared the buildings of Eyeglass. Four riders, indistinct against the sunset smear. Herb Cole started to yell a challenge, then held it. He wanted them to come in, wanted to know who they were and what urgent mission had sent them here.

Moments later the foursome had hauled rein in the yard and he saw that they were Walt Hubbard, Charlie Moss, and two other Bar H men. His first alarm subsided, but then, at the looks on their grim faces, the certainty of trouble returned. He said sharply: "What's wrong, Walt? What do you want?"

A ground breeze scattered the dust their broncos had raised. They fronted Cole in a semicircle, holding down their plunging, restive horses. Hubbard, the leader, answered with a face gone cold and hard as stone: "We want you, Cole. You should be able to guess why."

Cold disbelief settled in the Eyeglass owner. The change in Hubbard was complete; all the friendly tolerance of his attitude toward the man from below the border had melted and now his manner was as hostile as that of Charlie Moss, forking saddle beside him. As for the Bar H foreman, Charlie had a half-pleased look about him, as though at the justification of his own suspicions. It was Charlie Moss who said: "Better throw down your gun, mister."

Herb Cole shook his head. He had not touched the weapon in his holster, and he answered: "Not until you tell me what this is all about."

Next instant, a weapon in the hand of Hubbard winked sunlight, leveled at the man in the barn doorway. "Shed it, Cole!" the Bar H owner ordered harshly. "Or, rather, just stand hitched and keep your hands clear." Then, moving deliberately, he swung a stocky leg across saddle and came down, striding toward Cole.

The latter made no move as the rancher lifted his weapon out of leather, tossed it aside. Resistance would have been futile against Hubbard's drawn gun and the Colt that Charlie Moss now had unlimbered and leveled across his saddle horn. The other pair hadn't gone for weapons, but they would at the first hostile move.

"All right," he gritted. "Now, speak your piece. What the devil is this?"

Hubbard said shortly: "It's murder. We're takin' you for what you did to Jed Giboney."

For a long moment during which the world seemed to stand still about him, Cole could only stare, completely without comprehension of the thing he had heard. He stammered a little, forcing out words. "You mean, Giboney's . . . dead?"

Charlie Moss let out a disgusted snort. "Aw, hell, fellow! You can cut out the play-acting."

"But . . . but I tell you I don't know a blamed thing about it!" Temper was beginning to have its way with the Eyeglass owner, at the preposterous charge. "When was he killed, and where?"

Hubbard lifted his shoulders in a tired gesture. "It seems a waste of breath, telling you the details we're perfectly certain you already know. You waylaid Jed Giboney at the forks this afternoon, and shot him as he started down the arroyo trail to his ranch. What you apparently don't know is that he didn't die . . . not right away. He lived long enough to drag himself to the forks . . . and that must have been a long time, too, because Charlie and me had left town something like a half hour later than him, and yet we saw nothing of him. Ed Lister, there, found him dying with a trail of blood behind him and with strength left to get out three words before he passed out. Them three words was . . . *'Cole murdered me!'* "

They struck like hammer blows at the accused man's numbed brain. He shook his head a little dazedly. "He *couldn't* have said that."

Lister, an honest-looking sort of cowpuncher, replied flatly from his saddle: "I can't help it. That's just what he did say. A dyin' man don't lie. He'd been saving up those words and he put all he had in getting them out plain so I couldn't have misunderstood him. He went, right afterwards. I toted his corpse in to the ranch and told Walt."

"And that's the story," said Hubbard. He sounded like a very weary and disappointed man. "I've tried to keep an open mind about all this mess, Cole . . . even after that scene in town today. But I guess I know how wrong I've been all along the line. If you'd do murder, then I guess a little thing like cattle thieving wouldn't stop you. We're takin' you to jail."

Charlie Moss growled heavily: "Take a rope to him is what we ought to do."

"Enough of that talk, Charlie!" his boss cut him off sharply.

Herb Cole demanded: "Where's Sheriff Duncan? Making arrests is his job."

"He's still up on the rim, I guess," answered Hubbard. His eyes hardened. "Besides, we ain't so sure we'll want to leave this job up to him. We've sort of lost confidence in Duncan. We wouldn't like to see you given a second chance to beat it out ahead of the law."

An emptiness filled Herb Cole. So Lew Duncan was to suffer because of his faith in a falsely accused man. Somehow that fact was harder to accept even than the desperate situation in which he found himself. The unfairness of it put a kind of sickness inside him.

"You got anything to say?" he heard Walt Hubbard demanding sternly.

"Nothing . . . except that, despite all appearances, I didn't kill Giboney. I rode as far as the forks with Sheriff Duncan, and then I came home, and I've been working fence all the rest of the afternoon."

Charlie Moss said with heavy sarcasm: "I suppose you've got lots of witnesses."

"I haven't got any."

"And *we* got the one witness that counts," the man in the quill-worked vest lashed back at him. "The word of the gent you murdered."

Walt Hubbard cut in: "All right. Stop it. Let's be getting on the trail for town. Where's your bronc', Cole?"

The prisoner jerked his head toward the dark barn behind him. "In there," he said shortly.

"Bring him out, then. I'll be right behind you, Cole."

As the prisoner heeled about, reluctant but obedient to the other's drawn gun, the creak of saddle leather sounded and Charlie Moss came down off his bronco, moved forward. "I better go along, too, boss," he grunted suspiciously. "He's a tricky son-of-a-bitch."

Herb Cole went ahead of the Bar H pair into the dimness where pencil-thin shafts of late sunlight cut through dust swimming in the air. Their boots made a ragged sound across straw-littered dirt. Billy, still saddled as Cole had left him, raised his head and looked at the men with intelligent eyes.

Hubbard said—"Just a minute!"—and stepped around his prisoner, slid the Winchester from the scabbard on the saddle, and tossed it into a manger. He said: "That's better." He backed away, rejoining Charlie Moss with Colt revolver in hand. "All right, Cole. Bring him out."

But Herb Cole had caught sight of the axe handle, leaning

163

where he had placed it against a roof support. There was no time to think. Dropping Billy's reins, he took one quick stride and caught it up.

Even as he pivoted, lifting this crude weapon, Walt Hubbard took alarm and his Colt revolver let go with a blast of sound and muzzle flame. Somehow the bullet missed—Cole had put everything into a swing of the axe handle that he hoped might knock the gun off target. Instead, the revolver's hasty discharge had flung the cowman's arm upward; the axe handle, striking it, was deflected. In horror, Cole felt his blow land with full force, against the side of Hubbard's skull.

There was a glimpse of blood as the man stumbled backward, dropping the smoking weapon. Charlie Moss was close at his heels. Senses numbed by the gunshot, Cole could only stand motionless as the two collided directly in front of him, and went down in a tangle together.

164

XI

In that moment a terrible question flooded Herb Cole: *Had he killed Walt Hubbard?* Walt was a good man, the only person besides the sheriff to show any confidence in him or give him the benefit of an open mind. But there wasn't time to find the answer now, or even pick up the fallen gun. That single gunshot had roused the other Bar H riders, left outside the barn. Yells of alarm sounded out there. Ed Lister and the other man had left their saddles and were coming at a run, and at any instant Charlie Moss could free himself enough from his tangle with Hubbard's weight, to get at his own weapon.

Without more hesitation, Herb Cole flung aside the axe handle and was leaping for Billy's saddle, yelling the black into action. Billy bunched his muscles and was off at a run, ears flattened with terror at the recent thunder of the gunshot and the tang of cordite. Lifted into leather by that lunging start, Herb Cole flattened along the bronco's neck. The wide square of the double doors leaped toward him and he burst through, just clearing the opening, as the Bar H men started into the barn.

They tumbled out of the way of pounding hoofs. Back in the dark building, Charlie Moss was on his knees. He sent a bullet after the fugitive, but it missed widely. Then the black was strung out, and, as the buildings of the ranch flashed past, the guns spitting back there were quickly left behind. But this would not be for long. The Bar H men would be in saddle at once, and after him.

Cole used the spurs without mercy, asking Billy to give him everything he could in that brief moment of advantage surprise had granted him. He headed directly north, knowing

165

his only chance lay beyond the rim, in that tangled up-country.

He skirted the bread-loaf hill behind his ranch, losing sight of the cluttered buildings and, momentarily, of the barking guns. Then rolling grass swells lifted and fell in long, undulating lines beneath his bronco, and Billy's hoofs beat out their strong, unwavering rhythm. Herb Cole spoke encouragement to the black, saw the bronco's ears twitch to the sound of his voice. Billy knew what was needed of him.

The Bar H men were in saddle now, and, looking back, he could see them, spread out and coming fast, three dark shapes in the failing sunlight. Three. Then Walt Hubbard apparently was not badly enough hurt that any of his men needed to stay behind with him. Or—did it mean he was past all help? No way of knowing!

Despite the odds, he saw two things working in his favor. He was on his own range, familiar to him in every ridge and hollow, and the swift settling of dusk had already begun coming on the land as day faded. Shadows were lengthening, creeping out of the low places, spreading like a smoky haze that distorted the shapes of things. He had to make the most of this twilight period before the rising of the moon.

Charlie Moss and the Bar H men must have sensed the danger. Their guns began barking whenever the lift and fall of the blurring land gave them a glimpse of their target. Over his shoulder, Cole could see spurting muzzle flame against the deepening darkness. Once or twice a bullet came close enough to let him hear its deadly whine, but the distance was long for six-gun shooting and Billy was holding it.

Then, as the black dipped into a brushy ravine between two slanting slopes, Herb Cole saw a possibility, and he pulled sharply into the scrub growth, came down from saddle to crouch closely in the protection of the pooled shadows there. Tense seconds drew out. The drum of pursuing hoofs strengthened to crescendo; the trio of riders came in sight, stung out, silhouetting in quick succession over the bare brow of the hill he had just cleared.

They poured into the hollow and up the farther slope, so near to Herb Cole's hiding place that he could hear the grunting of their mounts, see the vague outlines of the riders—even the shape of Charlie Moss's leather vest snapping behind him with the speed of his mount. Almost before the last rider had dropped from view against the dimming sky, he was up again and sending Billy quickly through the brush, into the tilting V of the draw.

Once clear of the head of the ravine, he let Billy out in a new direction. For a brief while, at least, he had lost them, although they would see quickly enough through his trick and be doubling back, and getting the right trail. Meanwhile, however, with every passing second his lead was lengthening, and the shielding mantle of darkness settling closer upon the wide land.

With danger left behind for the moment and with the steady drum of Billy's hoofs beating their dull rhythm into his tired brain, full realization of the shape of things came bearing in upon Herb Cole, filling him with dark and futile thoughts. Jed Giboney—murdered, and with his last breath pinning the crime on an innocent man. As Ed Lister had grimly and truthfully said: no dying man—not even one like Giboney—would tell a lie. Old Jed had been sure of his murderer, and, wrong as he was, no one would be apt to doubt his deadly final words.

Night was full now. A single star made its brilliant scintillation in the west, and all around the dark bowl of earth the outlines of hill and tree and brush were sharp and distinct, as though cut from black cardboard and pasted against the sky.

167

This darkness was a welcome thing to a hunted man. But Billy was tiring and Cole halted him finally, keening the dark behind him while the bronco blew between his knees. No noise of drumming hoofs came on the night silence. He swung to earth, tested its sounding board with a carefully attuned ear, but no distant rumble came to him.

He straightened, drawing a long breath. "We lost 'em," he told Billy. "Thanks, fellow. It's all due to you."

The black stood nearly spent, tired head hanging. Herb Cole gave the steaming flank a grateful slap, and then proceeded to let out the cinches. As he did so, the bronco filled his lungs, snorting the air through dilated nostrils. Cole let him have five scant minutes to rest; afterwards, driven by pressure of danger, he tightened the latigos and swung astride again.

But this time, as he pointed Billy toward the lifting land below the rim breaks, he took it at an easier pace and without the wild rush of his first flight. Alert and ready, he felt that even if the pursuers should close in again, he could cope with and elude them, aided as he was by a thorough knowledge of the land. Billy had done his job; he wouldn't ask that kind of effort from him again, spent as he was. You could kill a horse that way.

He reached the rim, however, without further sight or sound of the men from Bar H. Cole knew this unfamiliar up-country better than most men. It did not take him long to gain the spot he wanted to make a camp, and let the tired black take his rest. Sheer rock lifted at his back here, and brush screened the grassy level at his feet. Below, the tumbled earth fell away under the white face of the moon that had now risen. There was no water, but otherwise it made an excellent vantage point with protection and with a wide sweep commanding the approach of any enemy.

He off-saddled and let Billy loose to graze at the thin grass. Then, climbing to a point where all the broken land before him lay, open and clear to his watchful eye, he settled back to put some uninterrupted thought on the desperateness of his situation.

First of all, of course, he had no food and no gun with which to hunt for any. With morning, the manhunters would be up here in force, knowing he must have sought the rim's protection. This time, with the death of Giboney and—perhaps—of Walt Hubbard to give the final impetus, they wouldn't let up until they were rid of him. Common sense told him it was useless to buck the set-up any longer. When Billy was rested, take him and push on—leave this range, leave Arizona, while he still had time and darkness on his side.

Yet he also knew he wasn't going to do it. The murder tag would follow him, wherever he went. He might, of course, sneak across the line to Mexico as he had done once before, but a certain belated stubbornness rose in him at the thought. He was through with running. Maybe, if he had stuck it out five years ago, he could have worked out a solution—beaten the truth out of the lying witness, Syd Raines, for example, while Raines was still alive to talk. Well, whoever was out to jinx him had done a thorough job, this time.

So he spent a fretful night in his makeshift hide-out, half waking even when he managed to sleep. He was up with gray morning, and made breakfast by jerking his belt buckle over to the next hole. Then he piled gear on Billy, cinched down the saddle, and had him ready for any need.

With the earliest light, riders were in the rim breaks. Cole watched them from his vantage point, dark figures that crossed open scab rock, or sifted through scrub growth with only an occasional gleam of reflected light, thrown back from gun metal or harness trappings, to hint at where they rode. The hunted man watched with keen intentness. If they found his sign, and it led them to his hiding place, then the game would be all up for him. But the last of the riders drifted on and out of his line of vision, and then there was no movement of any kind in the wide and tumbled rimrock.

He waited yet another hour, to make certain. After that, he got Billy and, hugging all possible concealment, began a cautious descent from the rim and into the range country below.

With every step, he knew, he rode with peril. The manhunters who combed the hills for him would not hesitate to shoot before asking questions. On the other hand, they certainly wouldn't be expecting him to leave the security of the rimrock—the risk he knew he had to take. He needed to see the spot near the trail forks where Jed Giboney had been shot down. There just might be some scrap of sign there, pointing a trail toward the real murderer. No one else was apt to look for or find it, because no one else would think to question a dying man's word. Herb Cole, however, knew he hadn't killed the old man, but, if he was going to find any proof, it would have to be done quickly, before the sign grew too cold or was obliterated.

On quitting the rim he swung westward, touching Ward graze. Here there were tangled arroyos and ridges that offered the maximum of coverage as he worked south toward the Denison trail. Yet with all his caution he almost rode straight into disaster, when cresting a bare ridge he unexpectedly raised a cavalcade of horsemen jingling toward him along the trough beyond.

Deep dust had muffled their hoof sound, for he had had no hint of them until he saw the long line of men and mounts— ten or eleven, he thought based on that one startled glance. Then he was pulling back hastily, cursing the mischance and conscious that he must have skylined himself there on the knife edge. Even as he did so, he heard the shout lifted from someone in that line of horsemen.

Knowing he had been spotted, he looked around desperately and, using the spurs, was quickly quartering back down the ridge, risking a spill as Billy took the steep going in lunging buck jumps. The only possible cover was a thin stand of piñon halfway down the slope, and he made for this, put the black in among the trees, and swung down instantly.

"Stand. Stand, boy," he grunted fiercely, a steadying hand on the bronco's neck. The thin trees only barely screened them, and any movement of the restive horse could surely be seen even at a distance, but Cole knew he couldn't hope to outrun that cavalcade of manhunters if they once got fairly on his trail.

Next moment a horseman topped the ridge, and another quickly joined him. They pulled rein to throw sweeping looks across the lower hills before them. Herb Cole, hardly daring to breathe, held frozen in the scant protection of the piñons, whispered tightly: "Please, now, boy. Hold still."

The sleek hide moved beneath his hand as Billy shifted his hoofs in the rubble, but then, almost as though he understood, the black went motionless. Through the scraggly branches Cole kept his keen watch on the pair at the top of the ridge. They were talking up there, holding debate.

Suddenly one made a gesture of disgust and ended the argument by jerking his bronco around and disappearing again down the far slope. The second rider hesitated, for one more survey that crossed Cole's hiding place and moved beyond across the tawny hills. Then he, too, dragged his mount and followed in the wake of his companion. The sharp edge of the ridge stood again as empty as it had been a moment before. Herb Cole eased breath from his tight chest.

They looked right at me, he thought in unbelieving relief. *But they never saw me because it didn't occur to them anyone could hide in such a place. Maybe they weren't too sure, in the first place, that they'd really spotted anything on the ridge. It didn't take much to satisfy them they hadn't.*

He waited out still another tense moment, making sure there would be no further inspection. Then he was in saddle again, and Billy was off at a quick pace down the trough below the ridge. His rider felt a good deal easier along the spine when a stony draw received him and its walls shut away the ridge where danger had threatened him so nearly. Luck, he decided, had not entirely deserted him.

The misadventure, however, had made him ride deeper onto Flying W graze than he had intended. Sometime later, grassy slopes opened ahead and a dun haze of lifted dust stained the sky. Cole halted as he saw a good-size bunch of cattle being held in a natural amphitheater of rounded hills.

He guessed at once that it was the Ward shipping herd, the beef that had been hazed off his own Eyeglass graze in response to his deadline. A rider showed out there against the stir of grazing steers, riding a slow circle to hold them on this cup of grass. Herb Cole, scanning the scene, could not discover more than one guard.

The size of that cavalcade back there had shown him, as nothing else could, just how completely all-out the range was going in its effort to run down the wanted man. Obviously every rider who could be spared from duty must be out combing the hills and the rim cap rock for him. Well, that actually helped narrow the odds against him, because the farther he rode from the broken country where the manhunters would be most apt to lay their search, he would be increasingly less likely to run into danger from them.

So thinking, he sent Billy forward, laying a wide circle

around the cup-held herd and working to keep the uneven contours of the ground between him and the guard. He had almost cleared the far south end of the cup when, riding unsuspectingly past a jagged outcropping of granite rock, he all at once heard a voice rasp hoarsely at his back:

"All right, Cole! I've got a carbine pointed square between your shoulders. It wouldn't bother me a little bit to shoot a murderer out of the saddle. So don't do nothing to tempt me! Just up your hands, and stand fast!"

XII

He could only sit as he was, motionless, as his captor moved out of hiding and circled to face him. This was a lean, grim-eyed cowpuncher that Herb Cole did not recognize. His sorrel showed a Flying W brand, however, tagging him for one of Betty Ward's crew. He had a carbine clamped under one elbow, finger crooked into the trigger guard, and he was just uneasy enough over this capture to make him dangerous. He spoke again in a tight voice: "Be awful careful. You make a break and I damn' well mean to stop you!"

Cole didn't answer, but he had no intention of tempting that nervous trigger finger. His own hands were raised shoulder high, right fist holding the long rein straps. The Ward man looked carefully for a weapon but, seeing that the prisoner's holster was empty and that he obviously had no gun on him, let a little of the tension run out of him. "All right," he grunted. "You can put 'em down." He became almost garrulous in his triumph. "You rode right into my hands. I saw you trying to sneak around the herd and I could tell a mile away you would come right past this rock. It couldn't have been easier to pick you off! What were you up to . . . scoutin' this holding for your gang to run into the hills? Damn you, Cole. . . ."

The prisoner cut him off. "What do you figure to do with me?" he demanded. There was resignation in his tone. Suddenly, with failure, the nervy strength on which he had been running drained away from him. He felt suddenly the way he must look—a gaunted, beaten man, beard-stubbled and shaky with the lapse of hours since he had last put food into his flat belly. It would soon be three meals that he had missed.

The other man seemed uncertain at his question. "I think I better take you in and let Miss Ward decide. We're short-handed, what with everybody out with the posses looking for you. Hate to leave this herd, though, with only one man to guard it. . . ." He gestured with the carbine. "Well, move ahead of me. Real easy."

"I haven't got any tricks in me," Herb Cole said dully. "So look out for that gun, will you?"

"Go on!" growled the cowpuncher.

He ordered his prisoner down into the grassy cup, toward the grazing cattle. The other guard, seeing them, quickly spurred forward, and he had a hand on his gun butt as he reined in, staring at Cole. The man with the carbine explained: "He's under control, Bob, and I'm takin' him in to headquarters. You'll be in charge here, all by yourself. If you see any of the boys, tell 'em the hunt's over. We've got Cole under wraps."

Bob said: "Watch him close, Harron! He's damned slippery."

There was no slipperiness left in Herb Cole, however, and the constant menace of that carbine muzzle trained at his back effectively forestalled any move he might have considered trying. Harron kept the horses at a slow walk in an excess of caution. At that pace, it took them a long time to cover the distance to Flying W headquarters and both men were in a sweat when they got there—the Ward cowpuncher from the strain of responsibility, and Cole from the constant dread of taut nerves jarring off a carbine slug into his helpless back.

He was almost glad, then, to see the ranch buildings—neat, white painted house shimmering brightly under the sky, barn with its red roof, large corrals, big bunkshack and cook house. It was a nice layout, and there were grass and flowers around the main house. Even in this dry summer, Betty Ward

175

managed somehow to keep a lawn growing.

The two horses lagged to a halt in the yard, and at first nothing happened. The corrals were empty; there was no movement about the buildings. Men and horses alike must have been drained off to supply the posses that were hunting Herb Cole through the tangled rim country. But after a long moment of stillness the screen door of the cook shack suddenly jangled open, and a warped old fellow with a bald head and with an apron tied around his waist stood squinting at them, one hand shielding his eyes. The cook let a single startled squawk, ducked inside for an instant, and came out again with a double-snouted shotgun.

He hobbled forward, lugging the weapon in a gnarled fist and yelling excitedly. His cries had brought someone hurrying out upon the shaded verandah of the house. Looking that way, Cole saw that it was the girl. She halted with one hand on the railing, another moving up toward her throat. Her face looked pale beneath the dark and tumbled curls.

"We got him!" the cook shouted. "We got the stinkin' murderer, Miss Betty!"

Herb Cole stirred in saddle. "All right," he said heavily. "So you got me. Now will you take this guy with the saddle gun off my back? He's too ready to start using it."

Harron began to curse him in a tight, strained voice. But Betty Ward had overcome her first startled surprise and she took over with calm decision. "It's all right, Jim," she said. "You did fine, bringing him in. Shorty, keep that shotgun ready just in case. And you, Mister Cole . . . will you kindly step down?"

Moving woodenly, the prisoner followed orders. The old cook was watching him like a hawk, not missing anything as Cole lifted his right leg across the cantle, came down heavily into the dust. Harron, meanwhile, had gone completely limp with his release from responsibility. He had let the carbine sag against the saddle swell and was mopping sweat from his face with his arm.

"Take him in the house," Betty told the cook. She turned to Harron: "You go find the sheriff, Jim. Bring him here as quick as you can."

Jim Harron dropped his arm, staring at her. "The sheriff?" he echoed. "But I dunno where to look."

"Neither do I," she admitted. "You'll have to hunt for him."

The cowpuncher looked doubtful. "And leave you and Shorty alone with this killer? And only one man out there at the herd. . . ."

"We'll make out all right," she insisted. "Just get started . . . please! Surely you'll be able to find Duncan, or somebody who knows where he is."

Reluctant though he was, Harron didn't argue further. He freed the prisoner's reins from his horn, leaned from saddle to knot them about a spoke of the verandah railing. Then he turned his sorrel and went spurring out of the yard.

Behind Cole, the bald-headed cook said: "You was told *in the house,* mister. Start walking!" Shorty had none of Jim Harron's tendency toward hysteria; he seemed perfectly sure of himself. He followed at a little distance as Herb Cole headed for the house under the steady warning of the shotgun's double snouts.

The wide steps thudded hollowly under brush-scarred boots, and then upon orders Cole shoved open the door and walked inside the big main room. Betty Ward trailed the two men inside.

It looked the way it had five years ago, when Betty's uncle was alive. Cole had been in the room a time or two back then, before the trouble started between him and his neighbors.

There were massive pieces of furniture, rawhide-bottomed chairs, an adobe fireplace at one end of the long room, a bear skin on the floor, Indian blankets making bright splashes of color. There were bowls of flowers and other touches that showed the work of Betty's hand.

She said: "I guess you'd better sit down, Mister Cole . . . over there, in that corner. Easier to keep an eye on you."

Without a word, Herb Cole did as he was told. He didn't know, until he hit the deep comfort of the leather-bound chair just how near exhaustion he was, from lack of food and from the hard strain of that unpredictable saddle gun boring at his back. He went limp, let his head fall against the back of the big chair. His eyes closed for a moment, and, when he opened them, he discovered the girl and the old cook regarding him.

Shorty observed: "He looks kind of peaked. You suppose he's been hurt?"

He took a step forward, as though to investigate, but the prisoner waved him back. "Just let me alone." Cole ran a hand across his face, down over the cuts and bruises and the day-old stubble of dark whisker. It was the girl who guessed the truth.

"How long since you've eaten?" she demanded suddenly.

He shrugged. "Seems like a month. It doesn't matter."

"Go, bring some of that cold beef you had left over, Shorty," the girl ordered quietly. "And some coffee."

Shorty looked dubious. "Can you manage him?" he grunted.

"That's all right." She stepped to a heavy table in the middle of the room, pulled open a drawer, and took out a small .38 revolver. She showed it to the old man, and laid it on the polished table top. "I can take care of myself. You go fetch that food . . . please. We can't let a man starve to death in our faces. Doesn't matter who he is, or what he's done."

The cook gave a shrug. "OK," he said reluctantly. He took the shotgun with him, crooked in the bend of an arm.

A silence threaded into the still air of the room. Herb Cole looked across at the girl, who was studying him with a frown. There was a question he had to ask, but it took a couple of tries for him to get it out. "How is . . . did Walt Hubbard die?"

She only stared coldly for a moment, while he waited in an agony of suspense. "Do you really care?" she demanded finally. Her tone was completely frosty.

"Please," he groaned. "Don't lecture me . . . just answer the question. I hit him harder than I meant to with that axe handle. It wasn't the time to gauge a blow, what with two guns on me and a couple more outside the barn, waiting. And I figured I had to make a break, if I ever hoped to prove I didn't murder Jed Giboney."

"Why don't you give up?" she demanded, lashing at him with a heavy scorn. "Every time you're caught with your hand in some new crime, you start talking about proving you were innocent. That piece of goods is getting awfully worn around the edges, Herb Cole."

A tiny muscle leaped tautly at the base of the man's clenched jaw, but he took this in silence. Then he said quietly: "I know you plumb despise me, and maybe I don't altogether blame you. Especially after the way I kissed you the other day. I despise myself for that. But . . . won't you please tell me the truth? Did I kill Walt Hubbard?"

For a moment he thought she would not answer him at all, but then with a jerk of her head she said shortly: "No . . . luckily you didn't. You gave him a concussion and he was unconscious for nearly three hours. Charlie Moss thought at first he was dead, but after the boys lost you on the rim they went back and found there was still life in him. The doctor

gave him a shock treatment and brought him out of it. It's a
real wonder, though."

A profound weakness went through Cole in his relief at
hearing this news. Not that it helped his own position any, of
course. They wouldn't have hung him any higher, even if
Hubbard had died. No, that wasn't it at all. He was resigned
now to the fate he knew awaited him at the end of a hang
rope. But it would have been harder to die, knowing as fine a
gent as Hubbard had been sacrificed vainly in the futile break
he had made for liberty in the Eyeglass barn.

When the food arrived, the prisoner needed no urging.
Sight and smell of it made his empty belly turn over inside
him. Shakily he went to work tearing at the sandwiches,
washing them down with draughts of the scalding coffee. For
the moment he almost forgot the others in the room, and
what lay ahead of him when Jim Harron should return with
the sheriff's posse. The food quickly built new strength in
him and, irrationally, a revival of hope. This was so strong
that, somehow, it was with only a mild start of surprise that he
glanced up and caught sight of Niobrara Jones, lounging
quite casually in the hall doorway.

Cole had been leaning to set the empty tray on the floor
beside the chair. He straightened slowly, hardly knowing
what to think. Betty and the old cook were unaware of the in-
truder. Niobrara looked past them, straight into Herb Cole's
eyes, and his wide mouth broke into an evil grin. He winked
elaborately. Then, pushing away from the edge of the door,
he brought his hand out from beneath his coat and the hide-
away gun gleamed faintly.

The outlaw said: "Howdy, folks."

Both the girl and the old cook whirled unbelievingly.

Niobrara's smile widened, showing all his yellowed stubs
of teeth. "Shouldn't leave your back door unlocked," he

chided them gently. He looked at the shotgun slanting from the crook of Shorty's arm, and then the muzzle of the revolver waggled a little suggestively. Shorty was no fool. He lifted his arm and the double-snouted weapon clattered to the floor-boards.

"Give it the boot," Niobrara ordered.

The shotgun skittered against the baseboard as the cook followed orders, and Jones looked satisfied. But now Betty Ward had recovered, and, white-faced and staring, she exclaimed: "Who are you?"

"Me?" Niobrara shrugged. "I'm the guy that come in the back door."

He moved a step into the room. Betty retreated before him, around a corner of the big table, one hand groping behind her along its edge. Then from his chair Herb Cole spoke quick warning. "A gun, Niobrara. On the table. . . ."

Betty whirled at that, and made a desperate lunge to scoop up the .38, but Niobrara was too quick for her. He shouldered her aside, snatched the little weapon, and looked at it with lip-wrinkling scorn. He dropped it into a capacious pocket of his over-size coat. "You can get hurt with one of these things."

The girl was struggling with furious words. Cole, who had risen to his feet, told her quickly: "You were awfully silly, Miss Ward, to try anything. I saw you were going to, and that's the only reason I spoke."

"Real gallant," sneered Niobrara. He jerked his head. "Well, come on, sonny. You're leavin' here while the leavin' is good."

Shorty found his voice. "That's right! Go with him. We'll get you another time. And now we know he did bring a lousy bunch of border jumpers with him from Mexico . . . because this is one of 'em!"

"Why, you skillet wrangler, you!" growled Niobrara, turning on him. "Just for that, I ought to. . . ."

"Let it go, Niobrara!" Herb Cole cut him off.

The old outlaw gave a shrug. "Suits me," he grunted. "I got no wish to palaver with these stiff-necked Flyin' W folks. I only came here to let 'em know there's beef stealers on the way, right now, to jump that shippin' herd of theirs and push it clean across the border . . . while everybody is out scourin' that rim country, lookin' for you. But I spotted your bronc' tied out front, and I had a feeling maybe I'd better move in easy first, and. . . ."

Herb Cole interrupted as a startled exclamation came from the girl: "What did you say . . . attacking the herd? Do you know for sure what you're talking about?"

"Hell, yes! I know a lot of things. I've been doing some prowling . . . especially since you kicked me off your place yesterday morning."

The younger man reddened. "I hope you know I'm sorry about that. I had you dead wrong. But now we've got to make tracks! Only one man is guarding that herd!"

"You don't mean that you'd go a step outta your way for these people . . . knowing what they think about you?"

But Cole was already out the door and crossing the shaded verandah, and the outlaw went after him without further argument.

Betty Ward called hastily: "*Wait!*" She had shown a mingling of emotions during that exchange. Plainly she had suddenly lost all her sure bearings and no longer knew what to believe.

Cole didn't have time to give her an answer. He leaped down the steps and was fumbling with the knot that held Billy to the verandah railing. Niobrara had passed him to get the tough-jawed gray he'd left behind the house, when Shorty's yelp sounded on the porch just above them: "You two crooks ain't going nowhere!"

"Shorty!" It was Betty Ward's voice at the doorway. She cried out then: "Don't . . . !"

Cole had time for no more than a glimpse at the shotgun in the old cook's hands, its double snouts slanted squarely down at him, then something drove into him, jarring him offside, a fraction of a second before the weapon laid its thunderous sound across the stillness. Billy neighed in terror. A rush of murderous shot split the air squarely above Herb Cole, as he landed flat on the dry grass below the verandah.

Dazed, he rolled and pushed to hands and knees. Shorty stood there above him, gaping at what the smoking shotgun in his hands had done. Betty Ward, with a cry of horror, was coming at a run down the steps. Within an arm's length of Cole, Niobrara Jones lay sprawled and writhing where the force of the shotgun's blast had struck him down.

XIII

Herb Cole got to the dying outlaw just as Betty Ward came, flinging herself to her knees beside him, a moan of horror in her throat. Cole himself was too choked to manage any sound, seeing the terrible havoc the shotgun blast had wreaked. But the outlaw opened eyes that were dulled with shock, and focused on the face of the younger man. His mouth twisted feebly into the snarling grimace that served him for a smile. "Wasn't time to . . . use a gun," he mumbled. "Did you get hurt, sonny?"

"You pushed me out of the way!" Cole exclaimed in a choked voice. "You took the blast that was meant for me!"

"Evens the score . . . for that night in Ciudad."

Niobrara tried to laugh, but it was a dreadful, rattling sound. He bent his head, looked down at himself, saw how one whole side of his sprawled body had been bloodily mangled by the shotgun charge. He grunted, his voice growing feebler: "Better take my gun. I won't need it any more, and you will. Because . . . I found out who's been the brains behind the rustling you was charged with . . . and, when I tell you his name, you'll begin to see the size of the fight you got on your hands. . . ."

Surprisingly it was Betty Ward who prompted him: "Who, Niobrara? Quick . . . tell us!" Not consciously, during the stress of that moment, did Cole register the change in her— the fact that she obviously no longer disbelieved him.

Words struggled on Niobrara's blood-flecked lips; his voice came fainter than before. "You're bucking nobody less than El Tigre himself." He frowned at the lack of comprehension in Cole's face. "You lived in Mexico . . . you've surely heard of El Tigre, ain't you, sonny?"

184

"Of course I've heard of him," Cole said. "I never was clear if he was a real man, or just a legend people made up stories about."

"Oh, he's real enough," the dying man assured him. "An *Americano*. I never heard his true name, but I've seen him . . . seen him just today up in that rim country . . . with some of his Mex crew. A black-shirted, black-headed son of Satan with black fur that runs clear out to the knuckles of his killer's hands. . . ."

Betty Ward got the identification a second ahead of Cole. She stared across Niobrara at him and her lips shaped the name—Bat Doran.

Cole nodded. "I guess this answers a lot of questions," he said then, thinking it out. "Brannon was only a front. El Tigre is the brains of the combination. Maybe he'd got tired of border jumping and wanted to settle some place where he could enjoy his loot. He could have made a deal with Hawg Brannon, and they got themselves a ranch with a yarn about an inheritance. They must actually have had their sights on my place. They arranged to frame me, or at least have me run out of the country. But Sheriff Duncan balked them in taking legal possession, so they bought the Blackmar spread adjoining and proceeded to take over the best of my graze. And when I showed up again, they figured now they had to get rid of me for good."

"Could be more to it than that, sonny," Niobrara put in, his voice a mere whisper, his hand clutching at Cole's sleeve. "Nobody hereabouts . . . not even the sheriff . . . knew El Tigre by sight. But you'd spent five years in that border country. Even though you didn't show any signs of placing him, he could never be sure. . . ." A taut convulsion broke off his words. He stiffened, eyes widening. The blood stood upon his lips.

"Niobrara . . . !" The cry tore from Herb Cole, but he knew the word fell on deaf ears. The outlaw had lived dubiously, and he had died now in the dust—with buckshot from a bald-headed cook's sawed-off ripping him to pieces. Somehow, in stillness, his ugly face seemed to lose some of its habitual wickedness.

Up on the verandah, Shorty had dropped his shotgun and was clutching the rail with both hands, trembling, and with tears of shame on his leathery cheeks. "I didn't know what I was doin'," he babbled across the stillness. "I was all worked up and I just blazed away. . . ."

"Don't talk about it," Herb Cole cut him off. Suddenly the pressure was on him. He saw Niobrara's snub-nosed Colt where it had fallen in the dirt, and he picked it up, coming to his feet. He said to the girl: "Do what you can for him. I got to reach that herd before they do."

"Why?" Betty Ward was beside him, her hand seizing his arm. "Why should you risk your life on my account . . . after all the harm I've done you? This isn't your fight."

He contradicted her: "But of course it's my fight. They've hurt my neighbors, and let me take the blame. I need a chance to turn that around . . . and this may be the only one I get."

She saw the determination in him, and she nodded. "All right. Wait while I get my pony."

"Nothing doing!" Cole turned away, jerked loose Billy's reins. "But if the sheriff shows up, tell him all hell's due to bust loose out at that shipping gather!"

He didn't wait for argument. He was already lifting into saddle, and pulling away from the ranch headquarters with Billy stretching out to the touch of steel along his flanks.

Niobrara's Colt was the same caliber as the one Cole had lost making his getaway in the barn at Eyeglass. That meant there would be plenty of ammunition for it in the filled loops of the cartridge belt about his waist. As he rode, he checked the mechanism of the gun and its loads, and took the precaution to slip a shell into the sixth chamber that Niobrara had customarily carried empty for the firing pin to rest on. Then he slipped it into his holster, ready.

Within the next hour or so, he knew, he would need all the firepower a single revolver could possibly give him—for this was a showdown, and the odds would be heavy.

Herb Cole had covered perhaps half the distance to the flat where the herd was held when he suddenly caught sight of dust boiling against the sky, perhaps a mile to the north of him. He knew at once what this meant. From the speed and the direction of their travel, he could guess that these were some of the manhunters.

Hurriedly he swerved Billy aside and into the mouth of a draw, heart in his throat at thought that he might have been seen. Those men would be short-tempered after the long chase he had led them. They would have guns ready to start working instantly at sight of their quarry, and they wouldn't worry too much about shooting to kill. What supreme irony, to have them overtake him—now.

But with the very next breath, a startlingly different thought presented itself, and Herb Cole was hauling Billy's reins as the dangerous idea struck home. Picturing that shipping herd with its single guard, and the raid that might even then be under way, he suddenly saw the opportunity that had been given him.

Deliberately he turned the black and spurred him up out of the draw again, and over the round of a dry slope where a faint, hot wind stirred the sear grasses. He rode onto this open knob, and pulled in, forced himself to sit his saddle, motionless, waiting there for long moments.

He thought, at first, the riders below had failed to spot his silhouette. He had even pulled his gun with the idea of throwing off a shot or two into the sky and drawing attention, when he saw the van of the group wheel sharply and veer in his direction. At once he shot the spurs home and dropped once more down the far side of the knob, knowing he was cutting it fine.

He came off the rise and went galloping down a long and gentle chute. Near the bottom of it he glanced behind, just as the pack of manhunters poured over the crest in a tide of mounts and riders. They came yelling and whooping, and at once guns were snapping flatly across the narrowing distance. A rifle bullet whined hornet-like past the fugitive and he felt his shoulder muscles bunch together. He wondered in panic if he had let them get too close?

For now the ground lifted sharply under Billy and he lagged, the posse at once sweeping nearer. A rifle bullet struck the earth only a yard to the right of the laboring black. But then pursuers hit the rise themselves and this slowed them. With Cole grunting encouragement, Billy held that lead.

Again and again guns spoke behind him, without effect—the saddle of a running horse is not the best place for accurate firing. It couldn't have kept up long like that, however. Billy was already beginning to falter a little when, suddenly, the tawny hills dropped away. There, above the grassy holding grounds, dust was billowing—and other guns were sounding.

Raiders had struck here within a matter of minutes. Cole had expected the lone Flying W guard to have gone down at the very outset, but somehow he seemed to have got into cover of a boulder pile and was working a gun from there, unable to prevent the stampeding of the cattle but still putting up a valiant defense. A pair of the raiders—swarthy men on *charro* saddles, at least one with a bandolier of rifle bullets slung around him—were trying to knock him out of his position.

Upon this scene, Herb Cole came spurring recklessly with Niobrara's six-gun bucking against his palm. The two harassing the cowpuncher in the rocks were nearest to him, and they whirled. A bullet burned along his arm just below the elbow, breaking the skin. He threw a shot and had better luck. His slug dumped one of the scrubby Mexican cayuses, catching the rider beneath its weight; the man cried out as he felt himself going down.

The other cursed, fought a frightened bronco while he tried to level at the cowman plunging toward him. Then, as suddenly, he changed his mind. Cole was close enough actually to see the fear and astonishment flood into his swarthy features, for now the man was staring past him toward a perfect cloud of horsemen that had all at once poured out of a gap in the low, rimming hills. That *bandido* was no fool. Jerking his bronco around, he fled from there.

Herb Cole set spurs and went ahead, into the sifting and rising dust of the running cattle, his whole mind insanely intent on one purpose. There was confusion all about him now. The raid was turning quickly into a fiasco. Part of the rustlers had caught sight of the horsemen drumming in upon them and were breaking and scattering before them. Others, blinded in dust and deafened by the thunder of the cattle they were driving, stuck to their posts, and these were quickly overwhelmed.

But Herb Cole gave little attention to any of this. He lunged through the dust swirl, pulling aside once to avoid a scrambling bronco and rider, shouldering Billy past scattering, terror-stricken cattle—searching.

Then, suddenly, he glimpsed a pair that had broken clear and were hastening to make their escape. They had, in fact, almost reached the screen of cottonwoods along a sandy watercourse when Cole, battling free, first sighted them.

Brannon rode in the lead, working with a quirt to whip speed from his running horse; the man Cole had known as Bat Doran followed yards behind. They would have been into the trees and clearly gone from there in another moment.

But Cole had seen them, and, although Billy was tiring fast, he asked for and got from the black a renewed burst of speed that took him head-on toward the twinkling line of cottonwoods into which the pair had vanished.

He came under the cottonwoods and saw that his enemies had galloped straight up the steep-sided bed of the shallow stream that was little more than a series of mud holes in this dry season. Billy's hoofs alternately struck silver spray, then slipped in the slick, sandy bottom, but he drove straight ahead, although his powerful lungs were straining now and foam blew back from his nostrils and stung his rider's face. Cole couldn't see his quarry any more, but deep prints in oozing sand and mud told him how close he was upon them.

Where they had left the stream and turned aside up a narrow, boulder-walled cut, Cole followed unerringly. This had been a tributary of the stream in wetter seasons. It tilted steeply upward, and its dry bottom was thick with rounded pebbles that made a low clatter beneath Billy's irons. Cole was forced to pull in a little here because a bronco had to fight those rolling pebbles. He had been reduced almost to a slow and plodding climb when he came around a good-size boulder—and face to face with Bat Doran, sitting the saddle of a lathered horse, a revolver leveled.

Cole pulled up sharply, starting a convulsive movement toward the weapon he had holstered while he used both hands on the reins. He froze like that, to a warning from the man with the gun: "I don't think you're *that* stupid! Keep both those hands high."

190

XIV

They had turned, and waited for him—in a trap he had been in too much haste to anticipate. Frank Brannon sat his horse a few yards farther along the pebbled, tree-shadowed draw. He, too, held a gun, but it was in his lap, ready when needed.

"And, so we stub our toes on you again," Doran was saying. "Well, this will be the last time."

"I agree with you there," Herb Cole answered. "Whatever plan you've been following, it's finished for good now, Doran. Or, El Tigre . . . or whatever name you like to be called."

The hard eyes narrowed. "So, I was right . . . you *did* know me?"

"No, but I ran into someone who did. If a little late, maybe."

"Too late to do *you* any good," the other assured him. "You've been the wild card in this game from the start. The yarn I paid Syd Raines good money to tell should have put you behind bars . . . except for that damned sheriff tipping you off, and sneaking you out of the country. So, not long ago, Raines threatened to renege on his story. Rather than pay blackmail, I had to see that he got his needings in a barroom free-for-all. The next thing I knew, here you were, back again . . . a free man, and getting in the way of everything I'd been working for."

Doran had been growing angrier with every word, but now, oddly, his manner changed. Suddenly a half smile lifted a corner of his mouth, his tone became almost genial. "But, what the hell! I ain't one to hold grudges. I figure we all do what we have to. For old Brannon, though, it's different . . .

he don't forgive that easy. Since you scarred up his face and kicked him into the street the other day in town, he hasn't thought of anything much but fixing you for it . . . and I don't see any reason now why he shouldn't have his way. So . . . all right, Frank!" Doran said it over his shoulder and deliberately shoved his own gun into its holster. "Here's what you been waiting for. I *give* him to you."

At that moment Herb Cole put in motion the desperate plan of action that he had settled on. It lay beyond the realm of sense—trying for a break with both those guns against him, but he was staring at death anyway and nothing could be worse than sitting still to watch it come. Herb Cole thought— *Sorry Billy!*—and then his left leg jerked sharply, jabbing spur into the black.

With the movement he had hurled his body to the left, and this and the sideward jump of Billy, squealing to the jab of the steel, carried him bodily out of saddle. As he dropped, Doran's curse and the roar of Brannon's gun sounded. A bullet cut the air above Cole's sprawled figure.

He hit heavily on the rounded pebbles with a jar that almost knocked from his hand the gun he had managed to claw from holster as he fell. It took him a split second to get his bearings—time enough for Brannon to overcome any surprise and send a second bullet pounding into the rocks close to Cole's body. Then, lying there on his left side, Herb Cole got off a shot of his own.

He aimed it at Brannon, although this was the least dangerous of his enemies, for at the moment Doran had his hands very full, managing his bronco. Billy's sideward jump had sent him plunging straight into the outlaw's roan, setting the other horse to plunging and rearing. Cole had planned this, and he knew it gave him maybe a matter of seconds to settle with Brannon.

He shot twice, targeting the B-in-a-Box owner's thick, well-dressed body. He had so discounted any hope of winning in this uneven duel that he was mildly astonished when the second bullet found its mark. Brannon's mouth, beneath its carefully trimmed mustache, opened on a screech. Brannon's head jerked back, and then he went sprawling and twisting out of the saddle.

At the same instant, El Tigre fired. Cole felt the solid blow of the bullet. It took him and smashed him back, hard, against the stones, and sent shock coursing through him. Sun-dappled cottonwood branches seemed to wheel for a moment against the far sky, and then he narrowed focus on the killer's dark face, as Doran prepared to finish him.

He didn't know where he found the strength to lift the gun, which was growing momentarily heavier in his numbing fingers. But he dragged it up, using both hands, and flat upon his back he fired straight upward at that hating, mocking face.

The pound of the gun bucking against his arm was the last he knew clearly.

This wasn't heaven, but it felt close to it. The bruising stones beneath him had given place to something that seemed infinitely soft, by contrast, but which really was the deep comfort of a bed.

He was in a bedroom of the Ward ranch house, and he had been there now—they told him—for nearly two days. They told him that, when searchers finally came upon the scene of the shooting, they thought at first it had been a total wipeout. It seemed impossible that anyone could have survived. By the time they got him here, and a doctor was brought, Herb Cole had seemingly lost enough blood to drain him dry. Still it turned out that El Tigre's bullet had somehow managed to miss any really vital organs. And so things stood.

Meanwhile, he had plenty of visitors. Nearly everybody of consequence on that range showed up, sooner or later, in the stream of people through the bedroom where he lay recuperating, with sunlight making a bright patch upon the carpet.

Charlie Moss had been one of these. He came in with Hubbard, his boss, and shifted from one scarred boot to the other with a look of extreme discomfort on his seamed and weathered face. "Aw, hell!" he growled fiercely, lantern jaw thrust forward. "I can't make it no easier on myself, however I might try and say it. I treated you like a dog, and now I'm feelin' like one myself."

The man in the bed didn't know what to say, not being one gifted with words in the best of circumstances. He had stammered as badly as the Bar H foreman, framing a reply. Then Walt Hubbard broke in.

Walt still looked a bit peaked himself, from the blow with the axe handle, but he waved aside Herb Cole's halting effort to apologize for that injury. "I figure a lot of mistakes were made," he grunted. "So many I reckon it'd be best if we'd just forget 'em and start new again . . . where we were that afternoon in front of the post office. So. . . ." He thrust forward a rope-hardened palm, and he grinned. "Howdy, Herb. Welcome home!"

Lew Duncan was the last visitor in the late golden light of evening. He sat tiredly in a chair by the bed and pieced together the scraps of what Cole had learned from other sources.

"We got the whole story outta Brannon," he said. "He couldn't talk fast enough to suit himself, when he thought he was due to die from that bullet. I think it some disappointed him to learn he'd live to serve his time in Yuma. Anyway, he told me he was there when Doran plugged Jed Giboney . . . didn't have no part in it himself, or so he keeps insisting.

194

Doran figured, rightly enough, the killing would have been charged to you, even if the old devil hadn't obliged him by naming you. Hell, we all knew the old fool was blind as a bat. I think he just jumped to conclusions. Brannon's also told me that him, and that El Tigre fellow, had big plans for B-in-a-Box. Doran figured on latching onto Giboney's range, and your Eyeglass. Later . . . I dunno how, but I guess he had it all planned out . . . he expected to help himself to the Flyin' W, put all that good range together into one prime cow spread . . . and then give up his freebootin' and live in style. He had real big ideas . . . only, things don't seem to have turned out that way."

Herb Cole said earnestly: "Lew, I don't have to tell you I'm grateful for everything you did to help me . . . especially when you had to sort of bend the law, doing it. I'm just sorry I was so much trouble for you."

The sheriff colored with embarrassment, and ran a fleshy palm over his bald spot. "That's all right. I'm such a stubborn cuss, it was worth it being able now to remind folks . . . 'I told you so!' "

Betty Ward was in the doorway then to announce: "The patient's had enough talk for one day, Sheriff. That's the orders the doctor left."

Duncan shoved to his feet, picking his hat off the brass bedpost. "I'll be back," he said. "You get well, boy . . . you're still five years behind in your work on that Eyeglass spread. Oh, and one other thing. That friend of yours . . . that Niobrara fellow, God rest his soul. I'm seeing to it he gets a regular burying, tombstone and everything . . . if I have to do it with county funds. But there's just one thing . . . damned if I know how to spell Niobrara."

Herb Cole smiled. "It's no problem. His real name was William."

"Thanks. I guess I can handle that."

When the lawman was gone, Cole lay back on the pillows in the relaxed contentment of convalescence. Betty Ward returned after a moment, from seeing Lew Duncan to the door. She stood beside the bed, smiling at him. "Tired?" she asked.

"Sure," he admitted. He added on an impulse raised in him at sight of the girl in her neat, bright house dress: "You know, what the sheriff said . . . he's right, Betty. I *have* missed out on five years, and it just ain't good. Because the worst of it is, I've missed five years of . . . knowing somebody like you."

She sobered instantly. "What makes you think you would have liked me? I haven't always been very nice . . . losing my temper . . . slapping people. . . ."

Betty leaned suddenly and kissed him on the cheek her palm had struck that first day in the sheriff's office. "There!" she exclaimed, blushing a little. "Now I feel better about that."

"Me, too," Herb Cole answered, grinning. "A lot better." His arm had slipped around her shoulders and he held her like that. "In fact, right this minute . . . I'd have to say that everything is just about perfect."

About the Author

D. B. Newton is the author of a number of notable Western novels. Born in Kansas City, Missouri, Newton went on to complete work for a Master's degree in history at the University of Missouri. From the time he first discovered Max Brand in Street and Smith's *Western Story Magazine*, he knew he wanted to be an author of Western fiction. He began contributing Western stories and novelettes to the Red Circle group of Western pulp magazines published by Newsstand in the late 1930s. During the Second World War, Newton served in the U.S. Army Engineers and fell in love with the central Oregon region when stationed there. He would later become a permanent resident of that state and Oregon frequently serves as the locale for many of his finest novels. As a client of the August Lenniger Literary Agency, Newton found that every time he switched publishers he was given a different byline by his agent. This complicated his visibility. Yet in notable novels from *Range Boss* (1949), the first original novel ever published in a modern paperback edition, through his impressive list of titles for the Double D series from Doubleday, *The Oregon Rifles*, *Crooked River Canyon*, and *Disaster Creek* among them, he produced a very special kind of Western story. What makes it so special is the combination of characters who seem real and about whom a reader comes to care a great deal and Newton's fundamental humanity, his realization early on (perhaps because of his study of history) that little that happened in the West was ever simple but rather made desperately complicated through the conjunction of numerous opposed forces working at cross purposes. Yet, through all of the turmoil on the frontier, a basic human decency did emerge. It was this that made the American frontier experience so profoundly unique and that produced many of the remarkable human beings to be found in the world of Newton's Western fiction. *Cultus Creek* will be his next Five Star Western.